Almost Heaven

Thomas N Kirkpatrick

ARPress
45 Dan Road Suite 5
Canton MA 02021
Hotline: 1(888) 821-0229
Fax: 1(508) 545-7580

Ordering Information:
Quantity sales. Special discounts are available on quantity purchases by corporations, associations, and others. For details, contact the publisher at the address above.

Printed in the United States of America.

ISBN-13:   Paperback   979-8-89389-507-0
                  eBook   979-8-89389-509-4
                  Hardback   979-8-89389-508-7

Library of Congress Control Number: 2024918889

Dedicated to My Sons Jason Thomas & Jeffery Welsh

Thomas N Kirkpatrick
Written 1980 to 2021

Introduction

When the hour brings stillness, even amid confusion, I think that many of us, if not all, have a private sanctuary hidden within our conscious being. Nothing complex or challenging to reach, just a state to which we can readily retreat and sort out the experience of life. Perhaps for most, it is an unnamed region that we find ourselves when deep in thought. It may be the product of meditation, contemplation, imagination, or whatever four or five-syllable words you choose. But it is accurate. It may not be a tangible substance, such as wood, stone, or iron, but to our spirits, it is an anchor to weight us to the realities of our lives. Despite our hopes and dreams, it is our escape within us, bearing a reality that can carry our hopes and dreams to truth. It becomes a vision without the physical eye, which empowers us to see beyond what is seen and view what can be. It is the bedrock of faith. Faith is the immeasurable substance that allows us to know God and accomplish things beyond our reach. If I have faith, then I can dream. If I can dream, then I have hope. If I have hope, then I can have a life worth living. My point of refuge then is called Ballengee. Ballengee is a small community tucked away in my imagination's rolling peaks and valleys.

Ballengee is the place where my imagination resides. I realize that you see me here or hear of me there, but in Ballengee, I resolve the questions of life. Perhaps it is a strange state of my choice to linger there, as Ballengee is a fictional place, but it also is the reality of my imagination. Ballengee is fashioned not by my dreams but by the realities of past reflections. I believe it is just, as all fiction is born in the truth. So, I shall define Ballengee as the small town my imagination lives within and manifests to you in my words.

I once was a truck driver, a navigator of an eighteen-wheeler trekking across the great backyard of America. Throughout my road adventures, I'm a non-denominational guy, so a large parking lot was a significant consideration for a church. That would get me in the door, but they had better preach the Bible if they wanted me to stay. It was exciting visiting all those churches across this great land.

One thing I found great interest in was a small church located in Lodi, CA. It was a Baptist church if my memory is correct. As I was leaving, I noticed a phone on the foyer wall with a sign beneath which read one thousand dollars a minute. I inquired with one of the members to learn that this phone was a direct line to God. I was impressed.

Since then, I have noticed the same phone with the sign one thousand dollars a minute in many churches across the country. In my inquiry, the answer is always the same—a long-distance call to God. My adventures finally brought me to the Church on the Knoll, located in the lovely community of Ballengee, West Virginia, the Almost Heaven. They, too, even in this small church of only twenty-four members, had that phone as a direct line to God. The only difference was that the price was only twenty-five cents. I asked why the difference and learned in Ballengee God is a local call. However, as I shared during the worship service, each member's personal testimony and witness further impacted me. I felt that I had been brought into a sacred family of God. The love of each for each was overwhelming. The welcome I felt was a measure beyond genuine.

I also found this to be true of the whole community of Ballengee. With my fellow members numbering only twenty-one hundred, I felt part of every life there. Perhaps I enjoy Ballengee most because of its simplicity. It is where folks have not strayed far from the moral fiber that binds society together. There is no question as to what is right or wrong. Our Heavenly Fathers placed the code in our hearts, and we deny not His wisdom. The elders here still lead, knowing that where there is a breath of life, there is duty. The young are taught early the joys of obedience and the despair of disobedience. Here, the woman loves her man, and the man serves his woman. It may sound like Ballengee is a perfect little town, but it is not. We do have our imperfections, our misfits, and our injustice. Yet, the foundations are seldom cracked, and love and forgiveness win the day. For here in Ballengee, the white horse still wins the race. I had then decided to settle down and become a citizen.

Sarah Abrams

Sarah Abrams is a dear, sweet elderly lady. For most of her years, Sarah has been deaf and unable to speak. But it was not always that way. I was introduced to Sarah Abrams, who is an inspiration to all in their trials of life. Her life is a witness to overcoming the imperfections that come upon us with seeming injustice.

Sarah was the daughter of a corn farmer named Joseph Abrams. After school, Sarah, the son that Joseph never had, would work in the fields with her father. Sarah would help in the harvest, gather the stalks, shuck the ears of corn, and help her mother store the corn. Sarah was gifted with a beautiful voice and an excellent ear for music. Her mother hoped that someday Sarah would sing in the opera or become a great gospel singer.

It has been said to me by many when Sarah would sing in the choir at Grace Baptist Church. It was as if an Angel had filled her voice. There is indeed a unique quality of a youthful voice that is unmatched. From what others have said, I believe the Angels of Heaven must have paused to listen as Sarah sang here on Earth.

Sarah, a child, had the fascination of youth to explore the world and stretch her imagination. She loved to go off and run through the fields and meadows around her around her father's farm and frolicked in his fields. I imagine she would sing and dance through fields of corn stalks and meadows filled with milkweeds. I certainly understand the desire to see newer places than where she had been.

Angus Miller is a cattle farmer, and in that field was a large Holstein bull named Bud. I have heard bulls care little for flutter about them, nervous creatures with little defense against the fox or panther. So I suspect when Bud saw Sarah dancing about, he became confused and reacted in defense. Bud charged Sarah, and she was caught beneath his hoofs and received a brutal hit on her head, splitting it open. Sarah lay there bleeding and unconscious long past dark before Joseph and Angus Miller found her. They took her to the hospital in Capital City, where the doctors worked to save her fragile life.

Sarah survived the injury, but from that day on, she was unable to speak or hear. The whole town of Ballengee gathered when Sarah returned from Capital City and welcomed her home. Sarah was filled with a smile once she saw the entire town coming to welcome her back.

I've seen people discontinue for a lot less. Wrap themselves up in a blanket of self-pity and stop living as if it were useless now that they had lost so much. We tend to count only our trials and not our blessings. Yet, I believe if anyone were to take an accurate inventory, they would find the blessings always outnumber the trials.

This tragedy was many more years ago than I have been on this earth, and I don't know the pain and suffering that Sarah must have gone through. I don't know if what came about was immediate or if it was a product of time. I know Sarah, as she is a regular at the Church on the Knoll and blesses us each Sunday. Sarah's talent was not her voice or her ear but her heart. Sarah became a great poet and often wrote of her greatest love, Jesus. The uniqueness of her talent was not in the fact that she wrote on paper but embroidered her words upon the cloth.

You can come to Ballengee and buy handkerchiefs with Sarah's poetry of praise sown upon it. Or a lampshade, a towel, or wash clothes. Every

Church in Ballengee has them. Who knows the value of her service to her Lord? Who knows how many hearts have been swayed or blessed by her words written to Jesus?

It is then through the simplicity of Ballengee that we have learned the simple truth of the Kingdom to come. That's when God guides, He also provides. Troubles rush upon us when we step out of our chosen path. But to those who muster one seed of faith, know that no matter how far we stray, the path home is never more than one step away. Though Sarah stepped out and lost so much of her dream and hope, she stepped back in and found her life. Here in Ballengee, it is never too late, in Almost Heaven, to find our way back home, for God is just a local call.

Caleb's Baptism

I enjoy the adventure, as I live not far from the old church, which sits on a knoll just above the Greenbrier River, flowing to the mighty sea. I like to go as early as possible to sit by the river and enjoy the peaceful sound of nomadic water. How fitting, I ponder, that a church should be built here. Great oceans are born from tiny rivers, and from small churches, great congregations are also born, such as that great one in the soon-to-come Kingdom of Heaven.

Along with the grand spirits that attend, the church is a storybook version of which authors and musicians have written and sung about. The church stands elevated upon the Knoll with a high steeple pointing toward the heavens. It is interesting to notice that as the steeple's shadow travels across the grassy ground, it is like a sundial to detect the ages. It is a church painted white with green trim. The old wooden building sports a new red shingled roof, which we all gathered to place upon the roof last summer. Inside, the one-room structure still has an old potbellied coal burner for heat in the winter and Hard Oak Pews with Burgundy-colored cushions. The church has no stained glass, but a few years back, purple-colored glass was installed. We have only about twenty-four members, and we've become a small family over the years. We all are involved in each other's victories and sorrows. I don't suppose it is better or worse than any other congregation, but the family at the Church on the Knoll is an anchor in stormy times.

Sunday Bible class is held at the back of the church with Brother John, our teacher. Brother John is also the elder of our church and full of wisdom from his many years. The young ones meet in the front with Sister Mary and share scriptures they have memorized the previous week. We don't have a pastor, but once a month, maybe twice, one visits our church and gives us the word each Sunday when we don't have a visiting preacher Brother Simms gives the message. . He is not dynamic, but the Word of God mightily inspires him.

This Sunday was special. Being a small community, when a wedding, funeral, or baptism comes along. It is an event. Events call for a covered dish meal immediately following the service. Caleb Hodge was baptized this Sunday, and the whole church family attended. If you knew Caleb, you'd understand the significance of this turning point in his life. Caleb's business is a very perky moonshine operation in the back hills surrounding Ballengee. Though a bit of shine never hurts anyone, the lifestyle it generates does not precisely fit in a church congregation. Homer Massy had been working and praying about Caleb for a long time, and the Holy Spirit had now begun His work. This Sunday, Caleb, Homer, and Brother Simms stood before us at his side and gave an account of his journey to the Cross of Salvation. Then we all gathered by the brook, and Brother Simms Baptized Caleb in the name of the Father, the Son, and the Holy Ghost. It was a marvelous thing to witness, and I am glad the Lord blessed me with the witness of Caleb's Baptism.

After the service, we gathered beneath the trees and enjoyed some of the county's best cooking. We ate, had fellowship, and then had an old fashioned Gospel sing, which I, being well known for my monotone voice, lip-synced. The Crawford brothers, Johnny, Willie, and Bob, led us while playing the guitar, violin, and accordion. They, with their booming voices, make a great trio.

With everyone fed, visited, and sung out, we slowly dispersed and went to bask in the Glorious Day the Lord had given each of us. As this is my sport, I was back down by the Greenbrier, sitting on a well-rounded rock musing.

Water suits well my musing sport. We drink water, cook with it, grow our gardens, and even wash in it. The very sound of it is a great accomplice to the flow of my thoughts. I've felt its excitement as it gushes across the shallow rocks in the Greenbrier River. I have been moved to power from its pounding along the shore of the mighty oceans. I sleep better as it dances across a tin roof. Now, it is a trekking sound, part of my thoughts while pondering Caleb's baptism. Indeed, there is more to water than an H and two O's, and today, Caleb was baptized in it.

Imagine that Caleb Hodge is baptized! I have known Caleb ever since. The spirits of the more loving would describe Caleb as just plain quarrelsome. I would say just plain mean. Caleb first bumped into me back at Ballengee Elementary School. He was more than just the school bully because no other bullies would mess with him. At first, I felt sorry and understanding of Caleb. He didn't have a mother or father. Caleb lived with his grandmother, and she was a sight to see. I cannot remember anything about her except she was always sitting on the porch chewing some Mail Pouch Tobacco. They lived up on Creamery Mountain, and I liked going up there, but I usually stayed away from the Hodge farm. Caleb beat me up a couple of times because I wouldn't give him my apple out of my lunch bucket. The other was because he wanted to impress my date for the High School Prom. If Caleb had known the attention I got from her, he would have found another target. But those were the early years, and since we both left the confines of school life, our paths parted.

Recently, for the last six or seven years, I have known Caleb best by his dog. Caleb was not the most handsome person, though I would not say he was ugly. He might have even been reasonably good-looking if his personality had not always been in the way. Caleb had also let himself go over the years; his features showed the ware. But his dog was an ugly creature. I remember the first time I saw his dog, Mott. My job at Lively's feed store would cause me to go to Caleb's place occasionally. He lived in the same house as when he grew up with his grandmother. But now, it was a rundown old wooden shack waiting for a match to set it off. The wood hadn't been painted in many years, and some boards were rotted away. The tin on the roof was a rusty red that streaked down onto the concrete slab of the porch. The front yard had every imaginable antique farm implement rusting away. The old house's back was a mountain of trash that hosted a tribe of cats and raccoons. Somehow, I would always picture a lower class of Lil Abner when I envisioned what I had seen in my mind. This picture sat about 100 yards from an old wooden fence atop a hill.

At the gate, with his cement-colored hair, stood Mott like a gargoyle guarding the passage. If Mott knew you, he would only snarl and bark a few times till a stream of cursing came from the house. If Mott didn't know you, well, you'd be lucky to escape without needing some serious medical attention. Mott was a huge dog. He was near the size of a calf. Mott only had one ear, the other torn off in a fight with a panther and no tail. The story goes, and I believe it to be accurate, that Caleb cut Mott's tail off in a fit of rage and beat him with it. I believe it because that sounds exactly like Caleb would do. Once, when I was at Caleb's, he took a tree branch to Mott and beat him senseless just because Mott was scratching fleas. I would, and maybe should, have come to some sort of rescue, but I have not been able to forget the beatings I have received from Caleb. Besides, Mott was no friend of mine, but I did feel very sorry for any animal to have to live in that mess at Caleb's house. But I guess Mott thought I was a friend in a sort of way because he never attacked me at the gate. I should be honored because the first time my boss, Tom Lively, went to Caleb's, he needed stitches at the town clinic. If it means anything, then at least Mott was more civil than his master, Caleb.

The events recorded in the Ballengee Record substantiate the following account as told to me by our small community's more reliable gossip channels. One evening, after a good brewing at the still, Caleb came home somewhat out of physical control from testing his stock. He stumbled into bed, knocking over the table and passing out on the bed. Normal enough, as we all know, except the kerosene lamp went to the floor and lit the place up. Caleb was too far gone to move and would have surely perished in the fire. With blazes quickly spreading throughout the house and smoke billowing out windows and doors, Mott charged in and drug Caleb out. That old shack lit the countryside up for miles around, and many folks came to aid in putting out the fire. Of course, by the time anyone arrived, nothing was left to be saved. They found a slightly toasted Caleb down by the creek and a charred Mott lying nearby on the ground. They got Caleb to the Hospital in Capital City, but nothing was to be done for old Mott.

It should have been a life-changing event for Caleb, and it was. He got even meaner than he was before. I suppose losing his only friend was more of a reason for his hatred than a cause to change his ways. Being less sensitive, I felt that, Oh well, you reap what you do. But Homer Massy is the kind of person that can find value in anyone. Homer was determined to bring Caleb to account for what he had been and get his life turned around. Homer would talk about Caleb all the time and would go out and visit Caleb often. It was more accessible now that

Mott no longer guarded the gate. I don't think Caleb took to Homer at first. But Homer wouldn't give in and kept sharing the Gospel of Jesus with him every chance he could.

At first, Homer told us that Caleb would get mad and threaten him. But as time passed and Homer kept going, Caleb would start listening. Then Caleb began to get angry again, but not at Homer, more at himself. Homer believed that is who Caleb had been mad at all along. The first time Homer said that to Caleb, he threw him out. But for an old fellow, Homer is a toughie, too. Homer would keep going back, visiting, praying, and seeking answers from God. Finally, Caleb snapped, went to his knees, and prayed for God's forgiveness. Homer said the man shook and truly desired to change his life and follow Jesus.

I know all things are possible through God, but I would never have suspected any potential change in Caleb. I have managed to break a few bad habits and know the difficulty it is. But from as long as I can remember, from those days back in grade school till now, Caleb has been just plain mean. Friends, I will not tell you, but that is a very long time. So when I first heard the news, I went straight to Homer and asked what finally turned Caleb around. I know that Homer has solicited prayers from the church. I know Homer Massy doesn't t do much without the guidance of the Holy Spirit. If you pray for God to move a mountain, it will be done. I also know it would be easier to move a mountain than Caleb Hodge. So I said to Homer, "I know it is the Holy Spirit that changes the hardest of hearts, but just what did you say that Caleb hadn't heard before?"

"Well, son," Homer told me, "It was Mott. I asked Caleb how come he treated Mott so poorly. Caleb said he was sorry about how he treated that dog and that he missed him very much. Caleb said if he had it to do over again, he would have treated Mott like a King. After all, Caleb said, the dog saved his life. Well, I told Caleb what was done was done. Old Mott loved you despite how you treated him, but it is past now, and you can't get that chance back. Then I told him that Jesus loves him much more than Mott ever could and that he died to save his life. And then I told Caleb that there is a vast difference here. Jesus offers him a chance to do it all over again. Jesus offers forgiveness and a cleansing of the wicked life of the past. Jesus offers an abundant life ahead and peace and rests at the end of the journey. Caleb thought about that for a moment, and then he broke. It was an amazing thing to witness, son."

Sitting here on this well-rounded rock by the river, I ponder this event, the Baptism of Caleb. It is amazing to see such a drastic change and conversion in someone-kind of like Paul's conversion on the Damascus Road. It could be one never knows, does one? I know this, and the evidence is clear that there is indeed a power greater than our own. There is a master plan not only for our lives but also for all life. All things will work for the Glory Of His Name in God's creation. What tragedies come our way is most of our own doing. But only God can reach down into the dregs of our workings and save us from the fate we so much deserve. We had better be careful when we judge these things in our minds. For all is the working of God's will. I know from where this river comes, and I know where it goes, and all it endures along the journey is necessary towards its end. So, as it is in life, each one is God's life from which it comes to where it shall return. It is a cycle in the Will of God, in the constant need of His cleansing water, His filling spirit, and the proof of fire. It is a blessing to us all when one chooses to abide by that truth. Such is Caleb's Baptism as well as our own.

Oh, by the way. That still of Caleb's. He sold his secret recipe to the NHRA. Check it out! They are using it as a fuel for their fast cars.

<u>Andrea</u>

It is another beautiful day here in Ballengee. The sun is shining its golden rays down upon us from the high perch of the noon. Shadows no longer lean to the east or the west but fall directly beneath their object of shape. I have just returned from my morning trip to the grocery. I planned this event to be an early morning thing, but I admit that shopping is a chore I dislike. Mr. Fred Medder, a quite meek man with a permanent smile and words spoken from a compassionate strength, is also a faithful member of the Church on the Knoll, running the local market that we call Medder's Market. I could go on for quite a spell telling about all the little things that cause my attitude to fail during my shopping adventures, but they are petty when I think about them. I cannot once remember enjoying the experience. Today, though, God took the time to remind me that He is everywhere.

During my venture through the checkout lane, which was always an impatient experience for me, I was captured behind a scraggly elderly lady. She was not dirty nor of a sour aroma, but her clothes and person were well worn. What became interesting to me was what and how she was purchasing. A dirty sack full of soda bottles was cradled on her hip by one arm. Slung on her other forearm were a large cloth purse and two cans of cat food in her hand.

Just my luck, as the day was nearly half spent, and now at the checkout counter, I have to endure the return of an un-numbered amount of bottles. It has always pained my understanding why grocery stores have multiple checkout lanes but only use one. Her turn came, and she slowly extracted the bottles from the dirty paper sack. There were some Dr. Pepper, Coca-Cola, and UN-Cola and beer bottles, which were not refundable. This assortment of glassware was of the apparent origin of a ditch. All were dirty, and some had dirt, liquid, or both inside. Under the scorn of the checkout clerk, the money was counted out one nickel at a time.

This transaction ultimately brought on the next. I was not stressed further as I had resigned from the event. Amazingly, the price of the cat food did not exceed the available funds from the bottle return. Great! I would not have to face the inner debate about whether I should pitch in. Don't I pay enough in taxes? The tattered lady opened her purse to place the cat food in. Who could not realize the condiment-sized ketchup packages that nearly filled her purse?

She noticed my scornful look and meekly said. "Kitty likes to disguise the taste of the cat food."

Anticipating my long-awaited turn, I looked around with my eyebrows raised. Does anyone feel my pain? It was then that I noticed Fred Medder standing behind me. Not surprisingly, Fred knew the lady by name.

"Miss Andrea, how are you today?" Fred inserted into my already long delay.

"Lovely Mr. Medder. It is a lovely day." Miss Andrea returned as Fred told her to wait for a moment.

In what promised to be more than just a moment, but surprisingly, just a few, a stock boy appeared with a bag full of groceries. It had never dawned upon me that the cat food and ketchup combined were Miss Andrea's diet. I just thought she had a weird cat.

It does not astound me that I, and many, still wonder about the miracles of Jesus. But here, in a moment unwillingly given, I've learned one of the secrets of feeding the five thousand. It's Jesus working through us that provides for those who hunger. Jesus blessed the loaves and fishes, but His disciples gathered and dispersed them. Jesus' blessing upon our work in His will causes His Kingdom to be glorified.

Some distance is traveled here to understand the identity of Jesus. Argue this thought, then. Jesus came from the Father as a man and remained as a spirit. Does He not live in and through us? So we live because He lives.

Fred performed a great act of human kindness, showing compassion, sympathy, and a great understanding of empathy. While I debated the contribution of a few pennies, and only for convenience, Fred allowed Miss Andrea to do for herself. He then added to her profit with his blessing. Fred's act of kindness is an excellent example of the work of Jesus. Well, Hey! It was the work of Jesus living through Fred.

It is hard, if not impossible, to live a Christ-like life. For the most part, we stumble and fall each day. Jesus expects us to live by His example but knows the frailties of our humanity. Why not? He created us and has endured our experience. He has made provision for our escape and return to His will. It is our salvation from sin. We must be careful that our salvation is not into sin. One has said, "Christians that feel they have acquired goodness in their life tend to punctuate the flaws in others. We must continually confess our sins and not that of our neighbors. None of us will arrive while we stand here in the abyss of the world. Not while we are still shackled to our flesh and living under the inheritance of our sinful nature. What, then, is our hope? Where could we go but to the Lord?

What, then, is the tie that binds? Not our love for each other. Our love is a flexible thing. Our love balances between our needs and wants. Our love has great moments of strength and disparate moments of weakness. But this is the verdict of our conviction placed upon us in the garden. We are only human. Praise God with a great Thanksgiving for the age of grace.

When I realize that those whom I admire the most, all those whom I detest the most, both before now and to come and those of the present, both those whom I know and those I know not and those who remain un-imagined, that the worst of each was placed upon the life of Jesus, the Christ, who assumed the debt of all, then there is nothing left of a soul but the potential for righteousness. It is very idealistic and not consistent with the reality of our love. But there is consistency, and our lives are stable. The consistency is found not in our love for God but in His love toward us.

There are in this world those who are shining lights of His truth. They know the meaning of love towards one another as they know the meaning of His love in their lives. Perhaps before we judge one another, we should qualify the righteousness of our filthy rags. Perhaps most of all, we should remember that we all are seen in the judgment of His piercing light and forgiven.

<u>Will You Walk With Me</u>

I read a short notice in today's hometown paper, The Ballengee record, that brought back some treasured memories. It's a small-town paper, and after all these years, you still can get a subscription for a mere twenty-five cents per copy. The article was posted near the last page, page three, to be exact. After reading it, I felt I should share it with you.

The story, as I have lived over and over again, finds a small-town boy romping through an innocent childhood, with the most significant fear being the darkness of his bedroom. That monster beneath the bed, the creak of an old wooden door shifting in the draft of a lonely night, stirs fear within a child's imagination. It is a wonderful time when a young boy does not realize the cares and trials ahead in adulthood. Childhood is an impressionable time when the spoken words of an adult are accepted as nothing less than truth. Children are willing beyond sound reason to accept the word of an adult. Small towns also award greater acceptance for friends. You go with what is offered, as there are fewer choices. I think this is good, as we learn to accept people as they are and not as we wish them to be. We also must be careful in our weaker moments as everyone knows who you are and what your father is. Reputation is a valuable commodity.

Back then, only the well-to-do had a TV; if one was to be seen, it was in the window of Lou's Five & Dime store. The TV was a significant curiosity, and if taken to town, I would have to be dragged from Lou's Five & Dime store window on Ball Street. Heroes seemed to be of greater dimension. You read about them and hear others speak of them, but the chance to see or meet one was extremely rare. I remember once the Governor came to Ballengee. He was passing through, but everyone lined the streets to see him pass. It was a big thing to happen in Ballengee, but it disappointed me. It was just a long limousine with a license plate that read number one. I was too small to see inside the car as it passed. I particularly appreciate waiting for what seemed an eternity for just a passing car. I would have watched instead TV.

Early spring one year, even before school had let out for summer, posters were all over town announcing the coming of a Billy Graham Crusade. I had heard of Billy Graham much as I had heard of Billy Sunday. I thought all traveling preachers were named Billy. I even thought they were related, perhaps as father and son. Billy Graham was one of those famous people right up there with the Governor. All one could hear was people talking about was how Billy Graham was coming to Capital City this summer. The excitement of going to the Capital and seeing an actual, famous person was as much a dream as I could have at that age. But there was no way we were going. Capital City was 80 miles away, and back then, that was a journey not to be taken lightly and required resources we could not afford. At least, that is what my parents said. I remember my Grandmother going to Capital City once, but that was for medical reasons.

There are five churches in Ballengee: Saint Joseph's Catholic Church, James Street Presbyterian Church, The Church on the Knoll, and Grace Baptist Church. I had never been to the Catholic Church but had visited the Methodist Church once. The preacher there was a neighbor, but we went to the Presbyterian Church. Our preacher, Rev. Wheeler, was a kind man with a smile and a warm handshake. It seemed he always went out of his way to speak to everyone each Sunday and always had a word for me. I liked him very much as most adults didn't have time for the little people, as I was often referred to. After those Billy Graham posters went up, he would talk about going to the Crusade every Sunday. It would get me excited, and I would dream about going on Sunday evenings when I went to bed. I don't think Rev. Wheeler could get enough people together to go, as he never said how we would get there.

My friend Johnny Crawford went to Grace Baptist Church, and they had a bus. He was going, and I tried to talk my parents into joining the Baptist Church. Come on, Dad, I would plea, we could go there just for the summer. But no, we had to go to our church. The time drew near, and Johnny invited me to go with him to the crusade on the Baptist bus. I was overwhelmed with the excitement of going to Capital City, the Crusade, and seeing a famous person like Billy Graham. My parents were also excited for me, and it was all set. My Dad gave me Five Dollars to spend the day we were to leave. Five Dollars! I had never seen so much money before!

When we all loaded on the bus, some folks had to stand. I wanted to stand, but Johnny and I were given seats near the front. I got to sit by the window. That was great now I could see all the countryside between Ballengee and Capital City. Before we pulled out, a man at the front of the bus stood and prayed to everyone. It was a short prayer asking God to protect us during our journey and revive our community. After the prayer, the bus began our trip, and the man in front led us all in some spunky Gospel songs. He was a very enthusiastic man, and I liked him. I thought maybe he was part of the crusade, so I asked Johnny who he was. Johnny said his name was Brother Ricky D and that he was the youth pastor of his church.

Later, other people got up and told stories of how God had helped them in their lives and changed them from the bad people they once were. The stories were neat to listen to; after each one, Brother Ricky D would say a prayer thanking God and lead us in another song. I had never experienced a long trip before, but this was more than I had ever imagined. I couldn't wait to see what the world outside of Ballengee looked like, and I did look out the window now and then, but the excitement inside the bus was of greater attention.

At the crusade, I was surrounded by more people than I could imagine existed. Cliff Barrows opened the service with prayer, and then a choir the size of the town of Ballengee sang. I felt as if the heavens had opened up, and all the Saints were singing at once. Then, some other folk spoke about what Jesus was doing worldwide, and Cliff Barrows returned. He talked for a while and then introduced George Beverly Shea. Mister Shea sang what has become my favorite gospel song, "How Great Thou Art." I had never heard anyone sing with such a powerful voice. To this day, I believe God Himself sang through the voice of George Beverly Shea. Then, at last, Billy Graham came to the front and began to speak.

First, I was taken in by the fame of this person. I had heard of Billy Graham all of my life. I had heard people talk about him, heard him on the radio, and read about him in the Ballengee Record. Now, I was in his presence, and he had become authentic, not just an icon like Roy Rogers or Captain Kangaroo. Billy Graham became real and much bigger than the mystic preceding him. I wanted so much to become a part of what Billy Graham was doing and the mighty God he spoke about that it overwhelmed me. I don't remember his message that day, but somewhere during it, I made the connection that my desire to be a part of his work was the model of the desire that I should have to be a part of God's. Through our lives, we are given an opportunity to hear the Gospel and follow Jesus with all our hearts. We will be taken up to see Jesus someday, much like I was now seeing Billy Graham.

Someday, our names will be read as part of the team. Oh, how sad it will be not to hear our name called. While dwelling on these thoughts, Billy Graham began his invitational at the end of his service. I felt as if my name was being called right then. But I was just a kid of ten years, lost in a mass of humanity and afraid. I had doubts that I could find my way. Suppose everyone left and went back to Ballengee without me. Yet I wanted to go and meet Billy Graham and his Friend Jesus.

We so often ponder our way past a present opportunity. So many times, I have heard the still call of His voice. Yet, I have paused and said I would seriously consider this plea. God's work moves forward and will be done. We can be apart, or we can bend with the wind. We are His Sheep and know His voice, and we have no reason to question other than our lack of faith. Oh, how this must hurt Him, who gave us His full measure of love. We shall never know the extent of that which we also deny ourselves. It is incomprehensible as the reward is unimaginable in that glorious day when our name is read aloud in the mass of humanity. How awesome the joy to hear "Well done, Thy good and Faithful Servant."

A hand rested on my shoulder, and in near tears, I looked up to see Brother Ricky D looking down at me. "Will you walk with me?" he asked. How did he know? Brother Ricky D, a man of God already in the Book of Life and serving the Lord, would ask me to go forward with him. He surely didn't need to go forward, yet he wanted me to go with him.

I wonder how often we have thought of reaching out to a stranger and asking them to walk to the altar with us. So many times during an invitational, I am drawn to the attention of a twisting and fidgeting soul. Yet, I shamefully admit I ponder my way past the opportunity. I have often wondered why an extra verse is sung during the invitational.

Perhaps a patient Father is waiting for some stubborn children? Another day, hour, minute, or second that one should wander through life lost and in peril of an eternity without God's Love. I could have been that tool used by God to Altar that lost one's future. I have squandered much of the talent that God has given me. Someday, the Lord shall hold an accounting of that talent.

Yes, Brother Ricky D, I shall go forward with you, for we are the sheep of His pasture and Sowers of His seed. For we are instruments of His Holy Spirit's work, and I shall not deny Him who denied me not upon the cross.

I read in Ballengee Record today that Brother Ricky D has gone home now. He's there where peace and joy abound. He's with His Father now, and I am very happy about that. I never met Brother Ricky D after that wonderful day at the Billy Graham Crusade. Our lives never again crossed. But I know we shall again someday meet as I am still walking with him. I am walking with His master, as He is also mine. I thank God so much for Brother Ricky D. In that pivotal moment, he shared his courage and walked with me down that wondrous road to Calvary, where I found the truth and was forever set free.

Be Not Afraid

"Peace I leave with you, my peace I give unto you: not as the world giveth, give I unto you. Let not your heart be troubled, neither let it be afraid"

(John 14:27 KJV)

Last Sunday was Easter Sunday, a special day that holds a reverent image upon the pages of my memory, an anchor in the landscape of my life's history. With special days like Easter or Christmas, I gauge the passing of the years. It seems Easter and Christmas hold special magic upon one's time as we stop to pause and inspect the memories of those who have passed. Easter has so much imagery embodying the occurrence that one cannot help but fill the soul with it. It is a time of renewal, both in nature and in man. A co-existent promise in the higher realm that life is still blooming anew rather than moving to a final gloom of disaster. The story of Easter itself is that of higher love, a God who loves His creation so much that He is willing to sacrifice His Son to save it. The Kingdom of God finds hope in this story of salvation; in those of ignorance, a message is found in need of sharing. Easter is a time when Nature and Man come together in the promise of a new birth of life. Easter is demonstrated in the bursting blossoms of spring and the exalted spirits of man.

Brother Simms spoke upon that thought at the Church on the Knoll, and I genuinely wish I could remember every word to share it with you. I shamefully admit that I cannot even remember the text Brother Simms used from God's word for my life. In Brother Simms' homespun way, he brought the message to us in a way that made us leave the service filled with joy and charged with the desire to follow the true light. The whole service that day was special. Special in that I, and I am sure the others, wish every Sunday could be such a fellowship of Blessing.

We gathered at the Church in the morning glow of sunrise with a Prayer of Thanksgiving that the tomb was found empty on this day so long ago. Brother John led us in Prayer, and before the Amen, Sister Mary added her praises. As she finished, we all, one by one, added our praise to glorify our Heavenly Father. It was a moving event that we, brothers and sisters of the church, should share such personal moments of His presence. I ponder what a wonderful life this would be if every day started similarly. And why does it not? Indeed, in Heaven, it shall be at the throne of our God and Father.

After the Morning Prayer, the table was set for a church breakfast. Now I want to tell you, my friends, that there is no better food to be found than what was served Easter Morning at the Church on the Knoll. There was more than I could describe, but I certainly devoured more than I should. I fixed a large plate with four cornbread biscuits spread out as a foundation. Upon them, I laid a heaping layer of country sausage gravy. On top of the gravy, I paced two farm-fresh scrambled eggs with cheese melting on them. Around the dripping sides of my plate lay long strips of pork bacon fried, crisp but not burnt. Slow-brewed coffee with natural cream thick in butterfat. Now that is what flavor is, folks. I could not resist, just could not resist, the homemade toasted bread dripping with Martha Lilly's blackberry preserves. It is a wonder that I could stay awake for the service, which may explain why I can't tell you more about Simms' message.

After the service, we gathered again in the rear, where the children searched for Easter Eggs. Plastic ones filled with little treats for the youngsters of our church family. As the laughter and joy of the hunt faded with the scarcity of Easter Eggs, Brother John led us in a parting prayer. It was, my friend, an Easter Morning without comparison, at least until next year if we are not already at home with our Heavenly Father.

I found myself committed to dedicating the rest of the day to complete laziness. Thus, I did, as I do so well, and found myself sitting up on the front porch. Here I sat, exercising my ankles, motivating the old rocker. The old rocker is a fantastic instrument of slothfulness and certainly one of man's most remarkable inventions. Mine was rescued from the old cabin I live in.

There is a path behind the old Lively Feed Store, where I now find my employment. It winds around the hill beneath the Crawford home and faints down the side of a hollow. There, I followed a small cow path leading to a small creek as a kid. Following the creek, as it slowly rises between two tall, wooded hills, it opens into a meadow filled with grass and wildflowers. The creek bares off to the meadow's lower side, and wild raspberries grow along the perimeter. An old, abandoned log cabin is on the backside of the meadow against a hill that shoots nearly straight up. One's imagination can fill the history of this log cabin at a moment's glance.

There are four rooms. The first is a living room in the middle of the cabin, which is divided between a bedroom and a dining room. The cabin's back is the kitchen, which still has its old wood-burning stove, kitchen counter, and a well pipe. A stairway to the two upper bedrooms is between the living room and dining room. Off to the right of the log cabin is the old outhouse for those private moments of meditation. In those early years at Ballengee, I often dreamed of returning someday, finding that log cabin, and moving in. Life there would be so peaceful.

In the years that have passed, I have felt I've paid my dues. I've done my bit and fought my battles. I sometimes feel that I have earned the peace in the meadow where that old log cabin stands.

I was fortunate to have purchased this homestead from the Lively family. With its roof gone and the porch collapsed, the old cabin barely had a path leading to it. Proudly, the old rocker rested upon the collapsed porch coated in green moss. On this Easter afternoon, I rediscovered it and employed it in my peaceful place of relaxation.

As I moved back and forth, so, too, my mind drifted in and out of today and yesterday. Days have passed, and the events that have brought me here and shaped me into who I am are lessons learned, and mistakes made. I've had my share of good. I've had my share of bad. There are times I am not sure about. I'm still trying to decide, and this is good too. But of the bad times, they don't seem so bad now. As time has moved, the stings of those events have mellowed. Then maybe knowing how they worked out has made it all right.

Brother John came by and saw me sitting on the porch, rocking. I think he saw the value of spending time this way and stopped and took a position on the porch swing. I know it must have been the call of leisure as Brother John usually found interesting things to converse over. But he said nothing beyond a greeting and moved back and forth on the swing. His presence interrupted my thoughts, and I began to wonder what he was wondering. I wondered if he was wondering what I was wondering, which was wondering what he was wondering. It became a quagmire for me, and I could not escape it. I suppose I should have asked, but I did not want to destroy the peace of this Sunday afternoon.

Willie Crawford came by and must have also seen the value of this un-active activity. Willie, too, stopped and joined our company. Willie could not be silent and was excited about the baseball game he had attended on Saturday. It was just a community baseball game.

Ballengee has a community team that belongs to the state league. I am sorry to report that we seldom make the playoffs. We are not a team that can be beaten easily, either. Today, we played the Talcott Trojans, a very tough team. As Willie reported, they were not tough enough to beat the Ballengee Bobcats.

As Brother John and I moved back and forth on the porch, Willie sat on the edge of the porch, resting his back against the column. Willie told us how the Trojans would get on base, and then they'd scored a run. It went back and forth throughout the game, resulting in the Bobcats beating the Trojans by one run. And Willie said it drove him mad. Willie was so afraid that the game would end without the Bobcats gaining that one run needed to win. With a splash of exasperation, Willie said that if only he knew how the game would end, he might have enjoyed it better.

I said Willie, that is the point of it. Not knowing that is the excitement of the game. Willie said he knew that was right, but this game overtook him. Now, Willie was stressed out and was glad to find a peaceful porch to relax on.

Willie sat there and nearly panted as Brother John and I continued to move back and forth. I found myself in near agreement with Willie that maybe if we did know the end, what we go through would not seem so bad. I then discovered that as Brother John and I moved back and forth, he and I wondered the same thing. Perhaps it is cheating, but then we could see the value in the efforts of our trials.

In his quiet, forbearing way, Brother John looked at Willie and said, Be not afraid, Willie, for in life, we do know the end. God has it all planned from the beginning to the glorious end. With all that comes our way, Willie works for good for those who love Him. And the Father sent us His Son, that the door to Heaven shall be opened to us if only we follow Him there. For He is the light we follow, and for all the trials we go through, He is there to sustain us. He defeated that which we fear the most, Willie, death. He arose from it that we might live through Him. So we know the ending, Willie, and we can choose our path to life or death. You need not worry, Willie, be not afraid, for we know our destination through Jesus. Keep your eyes on Him, Willie, and all we go through is but a moment before an eternity in glory with Jesus. Amen, Willie?

And Willie said, Amen.

<u>Gordy</u>

In the light of a new day, I find myself rambling down the path from my little cabin in the meadow. Again, it's the time of year when nature reveals her mystery from beneath the ground, where the seed has been hidden from us throughout the coldness of the winter. Now, as the sun climbs to its morning perch, just above the trees with their new leaves waving a howdy-do in the morning breeze, I am as if it happened just overnight, amazed at the beauty that unfolds around me with each step towards the hidden hamlet of Ballengee. I am not surprised, as a hint of the coming glory was displayed yesterday in the rose garden around the WW II memorial at the center of the courthouse yard. Their loosely knit rosebuds of red and yellow promised to burst open at a second's notice. Again, it shared the marvel of spring passing through the peaks and valleys surrounding Ballengee's hidden treasure beside the winding Greenbrier River. In that blessing, I ponder forth God's gift, spring, a rebirth of nature and man's hearts. I once again find myself excited to be alive.

I cannot help but admire the meadow as I wander down the path, how the rhododendrons have taken residence beneath the trees on the lower side of the meadow. They're colorful flowers of pastel purples, yellows, whites, and the velvety deep red ones that command the bunch. There is now green grass waving in the spring breeze. Blossoms of violets have risen above to herald their arrival. What meadow would be complete without the king of weed, the Dandy Lions, now speckled about with their golden yellow heads standing tall. The air is now flavored with the perfume of Honeysuckle, and the bees have come out of their winter hiding and are now busy drinking the sweet nectar of spring's generous drink. I think that spring is a promise from God that life shall go on for a spell longer and that someday, we will return to the Garden of Eden.

At work in the feed store, I miss the sounds of the children playing in the schoolyard across the street. The screams and laughter as they play volleyball or run about in a game of tag. The school bell rings to call them in class or an announcement over the loudspeaker. They now enjoy the time of spring break and will soon return to finish the year before their summer adventures begin. Some find themselves along the banks of the Greenbrier with a long pole in their hands, hoping to catch a bass or trout. Others sit on the shore and dangle their feet in the cool water, dreaming of a soon-to-come summer romance. Perhaps a meeting of their hearts at the 4-H summer camp where many children will spend time during the summer vacation.

Most of the older children find themselves on the farm helping, with the plowing and planting of spring. They fill the soil with seeds of corn, pole beans, cucumbers, tomatoes, and melons and sow the fields with hay for the livestock's winter feed. I am amused that the soil we quickly wash from produces the food we need to survive. We bury our seed in the furrows and patiently wait as we pray for God's miracle of life to appear. One day, from the mystery buried beneath our view, tiny sprouts arise from the soil to provide us with our substance for the coming year.

Yet in the silence of the playground still, Gordy stands at his post, as he does every day of the year except for Sundays. He is faithful to his task in our small community, and not once have I noticed him absent from the corner, standing next to a stack of newspapers. Every year, my memory shelters find Gordy selling the Ballengee Record on that corner.

One never really appreciates our dependence on each other until they are no longer there. Each day, from my view at the feed store, I see the same folks stop to buy a paper from Gordy. I wonder what they would do if one day he were not there. I am sure his absence would become a topic of concern in Ballengee, as the balance of our lives here would be tipped. Yet, taken for granted, his presence does not cause a stir, but his absence would be the news found in the papers he sells. Strange as that is, the truth is that each of us, great and small, is needed while less appreciated. I cross the street daily to receive the Ballengee Record, exchanging a greeting with Gordy and wishing him a good day. Where would I find a copy of the Ballengee Record if Gordy was not there?

Gordy is a portly fellow of small stature, and I imagine he was not the most handsome of lads as a boy. His round head and high cheekbones arch down to support an overbearing round and often red nose. His cheeks are indented; I suspect this is because of the loss of teeth to support them. Yet his front teeth are bucked, causing his upper lip to overlap the lower lip, which disturbs his speech. As a result, Gordy is a man of silence with few words that pass through his lips. Gordy is also slow and seems to comprehend well enough but cannot express his learning. His clothes are as worn as the years that have gathered upon him. Not many know, but I do, that Gordy lives in the basement of the Ballengee Record in the cold and damp winter and the summer's stagnant heat. But Gordy is never dirty, and his eyes are always bright.

Children can be the grandest angles and the worst of devils and have picked up on Gordy as an object for their amusement. At Gordy's expense, he is fun for the children, as they taunt and tease him each morning and afternoon on his corner of the schoolyard. I am sometimes angered that the children have forsaken their manners and have little regard for Gordy's feelings, but Gordy never seems to mind. Sadly, the children's abuse is the only attention he receives. Sadly, we as people need the attention of others so much that we even find comfort in their contempt.

It is the existence of Gordy, standing against the elements of nature, the abuse of the children while selling newspapers to very familiar strangers. I would feel sad for Gordy, angry with the children, and annoyed by those familiar strangers who would give Gordy no more than fifteen cents for a newspaper if I did not know Gordy's secret.

In my own mind, I have supposed that most of us look at the way the rest of us live. We study their position and determine ours to be better or worse, and we strive to empathize with those less fortunate and admiration for those of greater achievement. It's a way to gauge our advancement in life and extract some pride or shame for our accomplishments. In my idealistic mind, I believe, for the most part, we all work to be the best we can be at our station along the way. And if we are happy in our labors, then we have gained more than many, so I imagine it is this way for Gordy. He has achieved that, which he finds satisfying in knowing he is fulfilling an important position. Somehow, I feel that if Gordy were to live somewhere else than Ballengee, we both, Ballengee and he, would be at a loss.

It may seem out of place to mention Christmas here at the arrival of spring. But it comes to mind as I watch Gordy in the emptiness of his corner next to the school playground, without the children to taunt and tease him. As he stands there selling the Ballengee Record, I see inevitable loneliness in his stature without the children's presence.

Each year, Ballengee holds a community event that I think is unique to a town of our size. We are small enough that we can all participate without any being left out. There is a price to becoming a city, and we lose the wholeness of the community. We become distant fractions of the whole and lose touch with all the members. We have been stagnant in growth here in Ballengee; a few have moved in, and too many have moved away. We remain a family of families living together and have stayed in touch with those seeking their fortunes on the distant ground. At Christmas, the families of Ballengee come together to enjoy the gifts and share what we have with each other.

We are entertained by the beautiful music of the Bottoms Gospel Choir, which shares with us all that special music of the Christmas season. Each of the five Churches of Ballengee presents a short interpretation of the true meaning of Christmas. Of course, we feed ourselves well. The women of Ballengee spend the week prior preparing mountains of Christmas treats. Nolan Richardson comes down from his home on Eagles Perch with a dozen wild turkeys stuffed with the best dressing ever devoured by man. We listen to and sometimes join in with the Bottoms Gospel Choir's caroling. Ponder the thoughts and words of our spiritual leaders, enjoy a feast that has no comparison, surround ourselves with the blessings of a community of concern for each other, and watch the magic awaken in the hearts of our children.

As all the children know, Santa Claus will make a special visit to see everyone somewhere before they return to their homes. I am proud of that; even Saint Nick has realized the wonder found here in Ballengee. We have been faithful to hold this event on the same day each year for as long as I can remember. We should not want a mix-up on schedule to cause Santa to miss our gathering. Santa has never missed; he has been faithful and has come to visit us every year. I remember the wonder of it myself as a child. I was being hoisted up upon his knee, sitting there resting on his arm amid the winter smell of evergreen, sharing with him my hopes for Christmas and receiving a special gift made of carved wood. One year, I received a wooden Indian, which I treasure more than my other wooden gifts. It has remained with me to this day upon the mantel, along with other treasured childhood memories. Looking at it, I remember the joy I felt when Santa gave it to me. I believe that is the real gift that Santa brings, the joy, which is his magic.

All this comes to mind, Gordy and Christmas, as I watch him selling his papers across the street next to the school playground. I know how the children treat him and how others view him. Yet, I know him to be a man underappreciated for his gift to our little community here at Ballengee.

Several years back, Newt Harper, the editor of the Ballengee Record, bought a little piece of ground near Barger Springs, just off the hard road about twenty acres where Newt planned to raise some cattle. It is a nice piece of land tucked away in the woods. It is a good grass field in the summer and easy enough to get to in the winter. Newt soon came into Lively's Feed store to buy some salt blocks and a large tub for a well he had drilled. He asked me to take it to the basement of the Ballengee Record for him, Which I and did with Junior, who handles the deliveries at the feed store, would need help with that tub, so I went along to assist. It was an excellent opportunity to get out and see the folks in town.

We arrived at the Ballengee Record and carried the salt blocks to the basement. Then we wrestled the tub down the stairs and placed it along the back wall near Gordy's room. Junior rushed out to get some air while I lingered to catch my breath. After that, I started my journey back to the street, but I first discovered a very impressive thing in the room next to Gordy's. The floor was littered with wood chips, and the shelves were filled with wood-carved toys. The truth of Gordy came to me quickly at that moment.

We go through our lives and notice those around us, as we do, yet we never really know who they are. We go a long way on assumptions and prejudice and seem satisfied with a shallow interpretation of those around us. It takes a lifetime to know a man; perhaps this is why God waits until life here is over before His judgment. We never really know who each of us is until we all have been. Imagine that Gordy is really Santa Claus.

Harvey Banks

Here in Ballengee, it was another beautiful Sunday morning coming up. It is the fall season now, and the weather has turned chilly. I rose early this morning to build a fire in the old stone fireplace. I like to be curled up by the fireplace on these chilly days, listening to the snapping fire give its warmth. I remember those cold mornings after Dad had built a fire. I would toast and turn until my whole body was warm. As a kid, I took an empty milk carton, placed it on the fire, and watched the smoke come out of the open spout. Silly, I know, but I was amused by it. There is something very captivating about a fire. Three things capture my attention and rob me of the activity of those around me. A starlit night, a fire, and television, the latter being something I gave up many years ago. This morning, I enjoyed the warmth and created that image with the milk carton for my children to remember during the colder moments of their lives.

As the family came into the living room one by one to dust the sand from their eyes and toast and turn themselves by the fire, I had that old milk carton ready. Should anyone wish to find the same amusement I once had, I left no hint for its purpose. In the evening of the day, I set my chair close to the still-burning fire, staring at the milk carton. I could not resist taking it up and placing it on the fire.

The smoke danced out from the spout captured by the rising heat. It was carried away to places unknown to search for its destiny. Much as we did when we were children leaving the nest. Guided by the warmth of family, we charge into this world filled with hope and aspirations bound to build a good life and change the world. Everyone who has made the journey and those yet to go has a story to write on human history pages. Each part must have been played, without which we would not be as we are today.

Today, we gathered the family and me for our morning's journey to the Church on the Knoll. We marveled at the stunning beauty of the mountains standing in their glory in the Ballengee countryside. And those mountains! What beauty nature displays with the changing of the seasons. The leaves with gold, red, and orange colors display nature at its best. The leaves swell in the autumn breeze against the clear blue sky. A crisp air brings out the comfort of a treasured sweater snugly placed around the body. A nipping breeze at the ear and fingertips awakens the blood and invigorates the body. The faint smell of a wood stove burning off in the distance flavored the air with a scent from childhood memories of long ago. They were capturing us in a time of simpler means filled with joyful moments. Oh yes, fall is a favored time to be in the mountains. Hearing the voice of the wind as it whispers in the ear through the hollows of the mountains, "I am a mystery for you to explore." Perchance hiked up the path to a golden meadow beside a chattering brook, with the water swirling about the rounded stones as the water fleas skim across the ripples an opportunity to place the checkered tablecloth and open the famed picnic basket. Oh, the gooey peanut butter sandwiches with the apple jelly always collect in the corner of the mouth. Have a not-so-cold cola drink with a moon pie or a cream-filled oatmeal cookie for dessert. We strolled together, each exploring the sight of what an awesome God has given for our pleasure and stewardship.

This Sunday at the Church on the Knoll was unique, as Brother Simms had relinquished the pulpit to a former preacher from years gone by.

This Sunday, the word was to be given to us by the Reverend Harvey Banks. I had heard him preach once before several years passed down by the river near the bottoms. Harvey has come to visit us at the Church on the Knoll this Sunday, and I have looked forward to it since hearing of his visit.

Harvey is retired and lives in Hilldale, a community not far up the river from Ballengee. Hilldale is a small collection of cottages snuggled in a wooded area overlooking the Greenbrier River. The folks of Hilldale gather at a small store run by Junior Dunn each day and discuss the issues facing the world's leaders. Most folks there are retired, and their politics are from an era that was a simpler time to live if reviewed by them. The gray areas between the left and right were less definable, and you were either on one side or the other. Harvey was not always a resident of this community filled with politicians of leisure, as in his workdays, he lived in Abbeville.

Harvey's days in Abbeville were filled by his commitment to a prison ministry at Stonehouse Prison. Stonehouse, a Federal Prison, was the whole existence of Abbeville. Stonehouse is the focus of and the substance of Abbeville. Incredibly, the twenty-five hundred inmates of Stonehouse generated about twice that number living in Abbeville to support them.

At first, Harvey concentrated his ministry on the inmates only but later expanded it to the families of the inmates as well. This expansion caused Harvey to travel some; sometimes, he had to leave the state to visit family members. As Harvey's ministry continued to grow, he would have to visit inmates who had rejoined the society outside of Stonehouse. As a result of his travels, Harvey decided to start a tent revival crusade each time he was drawn away from Abbeville. It came about from Harvey meeting a bandleader, Preston Morgan, who had a rich baritone voice on one such trip. The two teamed together and formed the Morgan-Banks Evangelistic Tent Crusade.

As the years of this partnership rolled on and gained popularity, their tent crusades grew. Their crusade became a much-anticipated event to come into town. I first heard Harvey Banks preach at one of these tent crusades. I was there with Fred Medders, who invited me and is a childhood friend of Harvey. It was a stirring service, and many came to know the truth. I, too, was moved by the mighty baritone voice of Preston Morgan as he sang that glorious song Amazing Grace, and one could feel the power of God from every word that left Harvey's Bank's mouth. After the service, Fred and I spent some time with Harvey and Preston, and the magnificence of their personalities completely took me.

Much has happened since I last heard Harvey preach, and Fred Medders has told his story to me, and I share it with you now. Harvey Banks, who is now 76 years old, had a severe accident, as we call strokes here in Ballengee. While he was in the hospital in Capital City, he had surgery to replace a vein in his neck. During the operation, a clot broke loose and caused the accident. Harvey was left without the use of his left side and was not able to speak, understandably. Harvey also suffered short-term memory loss and was most times disorientated and needed constant aid in staying current. It is admirable that his wife Charlotte never left his bedside during the weeks he was in the hospital. Fred Medders visited Capitol City nearly every other day to check on Harvey. That is a task, as it is an eighty-mile trip each way. Charlotte and Fred were there to support Harvey, but they came from the experience encouraged, and Fred has told me Harvey's trial has enriched his life.

As Fred described and history proved, Harvey believed he would recover and preach again from the start of his ordeal. The doctors said

Harvey would make some recovery through therapy and hard work, but they would be minimal. Harvey's chances of walking again were slim, and with a walker at best, his speech abilities would not show much improvement. The loss of his tongue would make it challenging to pronounce most words. Also, memory loss may clear up as the mind can channel different routes. The doctors did not paint a possible picture of Harvey's dream of returning to the pulpit as a likely reality. So, Harvey's battle began, and he fought it with his faith.

Brother John gave me a definition of Faith. Faith is grabbing hold of something that is not there and holding on to it until it is there. It is what Harvey did, and he believed that he would once again return to preaching, and through his faith in that belief, he fought against the odds of the doctors' prognoses. It was not an easy battle for Harvey, and years of physical therapy showed very little progress as time passed on. Many therapists said this was the best they could do and walked away. Yet Harvey went on without them working the exercises he had been taught many hours of practicing words over and over again. At first, only those who were close could understand, and then, as the years passed, others could hear what Harvey was speaking. The trials of a step and falling into the supporting arms of Charlotte and Fred or the arms of their children who often came to help him. A step, then two and three, followed by a walk across the room. He was fighting one step, one word, and one thought at a time. He was constantly working on his memory, speaking a sentence without forgetting its meaning before the end. A phrase, a sentence, a paragraph at a time till the mind found new communication channels. Harvey never lost faith and refused to be discouraged, and those close to him were lifted along with Harvey as they shared in the celebration of each small victory born of many defeats.

This Sunday, amidst the handiwork of a great God, we went to the Church on the Knoll to witness another tremendous handy work of God's that Reverend Harvey Banks would preach His word to us all there.

I must tell you that if I were the only one to critique the abilities of Harvey's oratory, I would have said this speaker would have been better off having written his message on the pages of a book. The message lasted for fifteen minutes and could have been written on one page of a high school notebook. Knowing the story of his trial and what Harvey Banks had overcome, I was absorbed by each word Harvey spoke. He wasted neither a word nor expression and delivered his message from Isa. 40, verse 31 *"But those who hope in the LORD will renew their strength. They will soar on wings like eagles; they will run and not grow weary, they will walk and not be faith."*

As I now gaze into the fading flames of the milk carton in the fireplace, the real message of Harvey Banks begins to settle into my mind. Harvey started with an audience that was held captive and, in the end, captured the audience with a small gratification in tribute to a long and miraculous career in the service of his King. But the real story is found in the measure of Harvey's faith.

So many of us sit on the bench of our lives, wishing we could play a more significant part in the world. We sit there knowing we have a more significant part of ourselves to give and that if given a chance, we could make a difference in humanity's history. Yet, we fail to see the opportunity and wonder why we are not called. Have we not lived a life in preparation for a grander cause than just getting through this journey here? We must offer not more than our labors for food, shelter, and what leftovers we can contribute. The answer too often escapes many of us, and we remain on the search with the hope that someday our call will come. We are taught that each one is a member of the body, and we each have a vital part in performing, and sadly, we somehow miss what we are to do. I have spent so much time sitting in the pew waiting for my call and wondering if there's a place for me. How sad that opportunity constantly knocks upon our door, and we never seem to notice.

Harvey knew that accomplishment is not given but is taken, and he set out to make his way with nothing more than faith in what he was about to do. Harvey grabbed hold of a dream and lived as if it had come true. In the end, for Harvey, his dream did come true.

Harvey believed he could reach the hardest of souls with an act of faith, and he did. With faith, Harvey believed he could reach the inmates' families, and he did; with faith, Harvey believed he could reach whole communities with the gospel, and he did. With Faith, Harvey believed he could overcome the physical obstacles and return to his life's work, and he did. If our faith is only in the shallow water where our feet can stand on the ground, we will never know if we can swim. If we are to prove our faith in an Almighty God, then we must reach beyond the known capabilities, beyond what is believable, and live as if God has answered our prayer. How else can we prove the capabilities of our God and our belief in Him? We are then, as the smoke soars from the milk carton, lifted by the fire of our faith, reaching unimaginable heights, seeking His Glory as we go.

The Churn

It is a lovely Saturday morning in the quiet of Ballengee. I have finished an excellent breakfast with all the trimmings of a farm-fresh countenance. I found myself in an old habit that somehow wanted to relive the memories of my early childhood days and fix a meal equal to my mother's standard. I am somehow glad that I have missed the mark, yet I feel confident that I have come close. I would not want to surpass her ability, as I might lose the desire to try to achieve the measure again. I had an error in my preparations the day before at Medders Market. In my haste to come home, I grabbed what I thought was milk, only to discover later it was buttermilk. I have never cared for the taste of buttermilk and was reminded this morning of my dislike for it.

Sometimes, this little provocation, such as buttermilk taste, causes childhood memories to pop into the forefront of my mind. I suppose this is the way of saying, Hey! This moment is to be treasured, and we do not want it forgotten. You know as well as I that we consciously forget most of our lives. How many times have you wished you had kept a diary? Well, maybe you do. But I have never done so and often found myself wishing I had. So, I reckon the mind decides what is worth reviewing and brings it up now and again to ensure the thought doesn't fade with the years.

In the early years here in Ballengee, my family and I lived in a beautiful farmhouse on the outskirts of town. Today, it remains, but it has long ago become another family's residence. I pass their time and again and look about the home site and wonder what life is like now. Do the parents have the same joy of working the land as my father did? Are the children busy each morning with their farm chores? Are they gathering the eggs or milking the cow? Do they play in the hayloft and explore the wooded areas beyond the lower field? Have they been curious about the initials carved on the door in the upper bedroom? I thought maybe I should stop by sometime and introduce myself, but I never have. I wonder why they would probably find it interesting to learn what went on there so long ago.

The farmhouse was a log home built by Robert Ballengee's son, William, in the 1850s. It was built upon the ground that slopped off to the East, with the house facing the North. I remember how we could sit on the front porch and watch the sunlight travel from one side of the front yard to the other as it crossed the sky. Many a day, I started watching the sunrise and finished watching the sunset from the rocking chairs on the front porch. I do not think this is all we did, as each day had plenty to do. The ground to the east sloped down to a large field. I spent many days in that field hoisting hay bales onto the wagon and then taking it to the barn. To the back of the house were the chicken coop and hog pen. Farther down was the shed that had all the farm equipment. In the center was the outhouse, and behind it was a woodpile. On the Westside was a grape vineyard, which to the far side was the garden. To the North, the ground rose just beyond the hard road to a barnyard. To the right stood a large barn where the hay was stored for winter feed. On the left was an old schoolhouse where William Ballengee used to teach. In the middle was where an old Jersey cow named Ruby grazed.

In the earlier years, my mornings would always follow my father around, feeding the chickens in the coop behind the hog pen and down the hill. After feeding the chickens, pumping water into the troths for the cows, and ensuring there were salt blocks out for them, we'd return to the house for breakfast. After breakfast, Dad would gather the farmhands and plan the chores for the day. Sometimes, Dad would take me to plow a field or out to the upper farm where our cattle grazed. If it were bailing time, I'd be tossing the bales onto the wagon and transported to the barn across the hard road. I might find myself picking beans, shucking corn, and various other duties a boy could do. Other times, I'd go with my mother to milk Ruby. She tried to teach me how to milk Ruby, but I expected that the cow didn't like strange hands. I never could get more than a squirt, and once I was doing good, Ruby kicked the bucket over just so no one would know I had gotten any milk from her. To this day, it is a task I have never mastered. She was a good milk cow; we'd get a bucket full daily. I remember the first time I tasted milk from Ruby, and I thought it tasted terrible. Mom would secretly skim the butterfat off and tell me it was store-bought. For many years, I never guessed.

Mom would pour some of the milk from Ruby into a large churn and let it set till Saturday. Saturday was her day for churning the milk. It would sit there all week and curdle up and smell horrible. I couldn't believe how good the butter tasted after she was through churning. She'd also get buttermilk that I would never ever drink, but Dad and the other hands loved it. There is nothing like the taste of real butter, but the buttermilk tasted like I thought it should come from that old, smelly churn. I could never figure out how such a good-tasting butter could come from it. Nothing was better than sitting down to a meal with real cornbread soaking in real butter. That and red beans with ham hocks, snap beans, fried tomatoes, and sweet corn on the cob was lunch and held us up to the big feed at supper.

But today, the butter comes to mind as that mouth full of buttermilk jolted my mind back to those days on the farm. I remember how, right before mom churned, she'd take the cloth off the top of the churn, why the smell that came out of it would chase even the flies away. She'd start churning, pulling the stick with a flat surface with holes in it, up and down. She'd get to going, and the whole porch would bounce along with her. Now and then, she would stop, wipe her forehead, and holler, "Whew boy," throw in a pinch of salt and some sugar, and go again. When she was done, she'd dip the golden butter into separate mounds on plates and put it in the icebox. Then, some of it was thick-looking stuff, like buttermilk. The rest was a thin, white, yucky-looking mess she'd throw out. Now and then, she'd let me have a lick of butter, and it was all so good.

I now find myself musing about how something so good could come from that old, smelly churn. You couldn't get me close to that churn, and when I watched, sometimes it would splash on me, and I'd run for the rain barrel to wash it off. It was, to me, as bad as stepping on a fresh cow chip. But still, it never kept me from enjoying the butter that would come from it.

I think maybe there is a secret here in the workings of life. As we travel down the road to our destiny, we will have life troubles. Some we bring upon ourselves, and others are handed to us, and perhaps this is needed. A churning, a test of fire and faith, a discipline of preparation for the golden heavenly bodies we someday shall be. For in My Father's House, we are all prodigals. Yet, at home, where His light is, there is a place for each of us. But the road back is not easy, as nothing of value is free. Along the way, we endure the churning of our trials here through life. In the temperance of the churn for those who hold fast to their faith, the victory will be won. Is this not love? Does a Father give his child all he wants or teach him how to obtain all he needs? Which of these is the sweetness of love, and which is just the sour taste of buttermilk?

A Brighter Star

It has, I must say, been a beautiful day here in "Almost Heaven." Working at Tom Lively's feed store seemed to go faster than most Fridays. The mornings of every day go pretty quickly as the farmers come to pick up some feed or seed. They will walk around the store, look at our wears, and dream of the day they can afford the water tank for the animals, some new chicken wire for the coop, and salt blocks for the cattle. But afternoons pass by slowly, and my most important job is to find a job that keeps me busy so that the time will pass quickly, but the day seemed to move at a steady pace for a Friday. I was amazed as I did not have to climb into the old 52 Ford F1 pickup truck and make farm deliveries. There were no deliveries today to consume the time, and I was amazed when the five o'clock hour arrived, and Tom said: "Time to get." So I gathered my lunch bucket, tucked my sweater into the back of my bib overalls, and left for my journey to the little cabin in the meadow.

As I climbed up the path in the meadow, I could see the wisp of smoke coming from the iron stove chimney, promising me that Miss Mary had an excellent dinner cooking for my enjoyment with the kids. Friday generally is a great day to look forward to. The weekend follows and is a time of home chores and family adventure. It also ends with a trip to the Church on the Knoll to enjoy learning God's Word and fellowship with our family of the Church. People come early to the Church and stay late. We do that to share our past week and explore the week ahead. Sometimes, the Crawford boys and I sit around and speak of the old days of our youth. Then we listen to the younger sons and hear how the adventures of youth have changed. It is never long before Johnny Crawford will speak up and say to the kids, that's not the way it was when we were coming up. If we did the stuff you all are doing. we'd spend much time in the woodshed with our fathers.

But now, I find myself resting in the backyard between two maple trees, swinging in a hammock. Whoever planted those trees so many years ago must have had a hammock in their mind. The distance between them is just perfect for a hammock. Not only that, but they are also perfect for catching the backdraft of the wind as it reflects from the mountain behind the cabin. The wind comes up across the meadow, hits the mountain, and returns to the backyard. That backdraft is strong enough to cause the hammock to sway back and forth peacefully. I like that as I do not have to exercise my knees, moving the old rocker back and forth on the front porch. But that old rocker is my favorite sport despite the effort it requires.

As I lay there swaying in the hammock, I am fixed upon the stars in the heavens. Two things will rob my attention from everything else: a crackling fire and the stars in heaven. As I sway beneath the stars in my hammock, I marvel at the inherent beauty against a backdrop of blackness. I sometimes ponder the fact that the lack of stars has impoverished big cities. The glow of the artificial light hides the billions of stars that pass just above us each night and day. How sad that the city folk miss such grand artistry of God's creation and never get lost in its beauty.

I've never been one to learn the constellations so far away from my little cabin in the meadow. But I have formed my own from time to time, only not to find them again on the following evening's adventure of the night. When one of our dear sisters passed from this world to the greater one, the following evening, I found Jesus up there praying over the world below. It was astonishing that shortly after that discovery, spring rain came down, pelting the ground around me, as I quickly moved back to the cabin porch. I sat on the porch pondering if the Lord was shedding tears over the shape His creation below had fallen to.

As I looked into the heavens this evening at the stars twinkling above, I noticed again that some are brighter than others. I thought that maybe they were smaller than the brighter ones. Then I thought perhaps they were further away from Earth, and we could not see them either, But this evening, the thought that came to my mind is it's not the distance from Earth but the distance from the sun. That seemed to be satisfied as Miss Mary hollered out of the cabin, "Are you sleeping out there tonight?" I could, but now I gathered myself and returned to the cabin to spend time with the children.

Just as I was about to depart, I heard a familiar voice calling my name from the far side of the cabin. Why it was Brother Simms' voice, I hear. I walked around to the front of the cabin as he sat on the porch swing. It was a place to rest from his long climb up the path. Brother Simms is a little further along than I am, and it must be important if he makes the trip up the path in the meadow to see me. That path from the hard road to my cabin is a steady incline; for a man his age, that is tiresome. Brother Simms has only come up this way once before, and that was several years ago. If Brother Simms made that journey to chat with me, that would add great value to his visit. So I sat down in my rocker and looked at Brother Simms with my full attention.

The first time Brother Simms visited was shortly after he started to Pastor the Church on the Knoll. He was going around and meeting each member of the Church Family, and one Saturday, he climbed up the path and stayed most of the afternoon. Miss Mary had made us some fried bologna and cheese sandwiches, lemonade, and a push-up for dessert—a feast in itself and worthy of the Almost Heaven. Miss Mary didn't want the new Pastor to rush back down that path without some proper nourishment. It is always an interesting adventure to sit and listen to Brother Simms speak, whether on a Sunday or any other time of the week. As I have always said, he is not dynamic but inspiring.

I remember what he told me the first time he came to visit the little cabin those years ago. He wanted everyone to know where he had come from and where he wanted to lead us. It was very interesting to hear about his life adventures and the wisdom that poured out of him, and I learned a lot, not so much about him as myself and the changes I should make. That is what a Pastor does, and he leads his people spiritually.

Brother Simms came from a big Church in Capital City and admitted that it had become too much for him in the later years. Brother Simms didn't want to quit pastoring, but he just wanted to ease the burden of a big Church. He explained how the Church on the Knoll and its twenty-five members would be perfect for his abilities. Well, one cannot argue with a pastor. Certainly, that would be a sin of some sort. So I told him I was sure he would come to love the family of our Church, and they, in turn, would love him.

That prompted Brother Simms to tell me a story of the big Church he had just left. He said he had quite a different welcome there. Capitol City had a problem with homelessness there, and he was concerned for them. Elder Clint had given him a call from the big Church and decided to accept. Then he had second thoughts and decided to go incognito to the Church and see how they were. First, Brother Simms went to the Salvation Army and bought some worn clothes for a couple of weeks before he planned to visit. He had meant to wait longer before going, but Elder Clint called and said they needed him to start sooner than planned. Brother Simms agreed.

On his first Sunday at the big Church, Brother Simms dressed as a homeless person. It was wintertime, and he wore a greasy jacket that was not all that warm. Underneath the jacket, all he had was an undershirt with several holes. One of the knees of his britches had a broad path, and the other just a tear in the fabric. The soles were duct-taped to the leather for shoes, all scuffed up, and had no shoelaces. Brother Simms wanted to find out how his new congregation would receive him.

Before Brother Simms entered the Church, he took his store-bought teeth out, and when he smiled, he showed a lot of tongue. All the folks in the Church were marvelously dressed. The menfolk looked very dapper in their find Sunday suits. The ladies at their side in beautiful dresses, looking as if they were at a ball.

Brother Simms greeted everyone who would be welcomed and offered his hand for a shake. Few returned the gesture, and as he worked his way down to the front pew, he stopped at some stations and asked for pocket change to buy lunch. Most just glared, but he did gain .67 cents, enough for a hamburger and a small drink at the Valley Belle. He finally sat down in the front pew and waited for the service to begin. An Elder of the Church came up and told him he would have to move to the back of the Church and find a place to sit there. He recognized the voice as Elder Clint. As he got up to move to the back, he noticed that people stared at a distance but quickly turned away as he drew near them.

After the opening prayer and hymns were sung, Elder Clint took the pulpit and searched the crowd of the congregation. After a few moments, the Elder began to speak and said that the new Pastor would give them God's Word this Sunday. The Elder waited a moment more and asked if Reverend Simms was in the building.

Slowly, Brother Simms got up and started to make his way to the front of the Church to take command of the pulpit. All eyes stared in amazement as he walked up the aisle to the pulpit. Brother Simm's eyes were fixed upon Elder Clint, who had a look of horror on his face. When Brother Simms reached the pulpit, the Elder stepped aside and sat behind him.

Brother Simms greeted them with these words, "I Have come to this Church to preach the words of our Lord and Savior." ***Then He will also say to those on His left, Depart from Me, accursed ones, into the eternal*** fire ***which has been prepared for the devil and his angels; for I was hungry, and you gave Me nothing to eat; I was thirsty, and you gave Me nothing to drink; I was a stranger, and you did not invite Me in; naked, and you did not clothe Me; sick, and in prison, and you did not visit Me. Then they themselves also will answer, Lord, when did we see You hungry, or thirsty, or a stranger, or naked, or sick, or in prison, and did not take care of You? Then He will answer them, Truly I say to you, to the extent that you did not do it to one of the least of these, you did not do it to Me.*** (Matthew 25:41-45).

Brother Simms asked, "What will you say to Jesus?"

After Brother Simms left, I looked at Miss Mary and told her I thought I would spend the night in the hammock. As I lay in the Hammock swaying back and forth in the summer breeze, I say to myself that I got this one right about the bright stars and the dimmer ones. It is a question of distance. Perhaps the brighter stars in God's Kingdom are the saints closest to the Son.

A Walk with Clyde

As I shut the door to Homer Massey's '57 Studebaker coupe, I turned and gave a farewell wave. Homer put the car in gear and rumbled off towards his home down the hard road. It was a marvelous-looking car, Homer's Studebaker, A long, sleek body with fins rising up from the rear fenders, it was a two-seater with a storage area behind the bench seat and a console in the middle. It was a 232 cube V-8 engine with a nice roadster rumble sound exhaust humming down the road. It had a shiny black coat of paint with white fins on the rear. Oh! To have a car like that here in Ballengee's "Almost Heaven." I stood there and dreamed of having a car like that until the sound faded in the evening.

As I walked up the path to the meadow and the little cabin I called home, I reviewed the evening Homer and I had spent together at Clyde Hawken's farm on Creamery Mountains. It was surprisingly a pleasant evening, and we left Clyde a humbled and happier man than we first met him. It is always good to come and understand why people are the way they are. Too often, we are quick to judge a person and let the first judgment hold on and never change. They say that first impressions are lasting impressions, which may be true, but I say it is a shame.

As I sat down on the porch step, I realized it was later than I thought. The little woman has a tremendous roar that sometimes could last through breakfast. If I were to fix breakfast for myself, it would probably be a peanut butter sandwich with coffee for dessert. Tasty as that is, it lacks the proper attire for a Sunday. So I sat quietly, moved on to the rocker, and pondered the evening just past.

I first met Clyde Hawkins of Friday while at work at Lively's feed store. I had not worked at Lively's for a long time and had yet to meet all the farm folk living throughout the mountains surrounding Ballengee. Tom had to run down to the Ballengee Deposit to care for some banking business and left me alone as Junior was making deliveries. There I was, the king of the store, and in walks Clyde Hawkins. Most folks around Ballengee are pleasant, even on a bad day. I offered Clyde a cheerful greeting and received nothing but a snort. Much like that of a hog, but I kept that thought to myself. I tried again to be friendly and said, "It sure is a pleasant fall day. I love the color of the leaves and the new crispness of the cool air." Another snort was the reply.

"You got any traps big enough for a bobcat, sonny?" Clyde grumbled.

"No, Sir. You might try Bobbie's Hardware down the street. They might have some traps. We have some wire in the back if that would help you." I said with an aggravated calmness.

"No, It's just the only thing I can suggest." My replay.

"I don't need another wild chase." He snarled, did an about-face, and slammed the door on the way out.

The pleasantness of my day was gone, and it did not come back the rest of the day. Tom returned from the bank and asked how things were going, and I said it couldn't be better. Tom asked if I was sure, detecting a touch of sarcasm in my voice, and I borrowed an answer from Miss Mary. "I said everything is well."

When I got home that evening, I had determined that I wouldn't sit in my rocker and stew over the day, as it would not be worth the effort and would only make it worse than it already was. So I grabbed the Sears and Roebuck and went to the outhouse to sit on my throne. When I drove out of the outhouse with odiferous flavors, I returned to the little cabin only to see Homer Massey sitting in my rocker. It is impossible to be mad at Homer, but he was sitting in my rocker. Being courteous, I took to the porch swing and waited for Homer to say something.

Homer said I see you are not in the best of humor. All I could say is that I had a bad day. With a surely not-in-Ballengee approach, Homer said, "Well, tell me about it." So I did. I repeated my misadventure with Clyde and even added a few details that didn't happen.

Well, you know how a story grows with each telling. Homer said, well, it will all work out. You will see. I'll see you tomorrow, and we will talk more about Clyde. Not the correct answer, but I bid Homer a pleasant evening and said, see ya.

I barely had my Saturday morning chores done when I looked down the path, and Homer was coming up. A large German shepherd dog who looked like Meme Mim's dog was by his side. When Homer reached the little cabin, he said, this is Hank. So it was Meme Mim's dog. Homer said Meme was getting along in the years, and the dog was getting too much for her to handle. Homer said that he would take the dog off her hands and find a good place for him to live. Miss Meme was grateful to Homer, and now he had this dog. But I thought Homer was older than Meme and that it would be just as hard for him to care for Hank as well.

We went out into the meadow and threw a stick back and forth between Hank and us, and he had a big time chasing that stick. Soon, he could catch it in mid-air, and now he kept the stick away from us. Hank was wearing me out. I was wondering how much longer Homer would last. I kept saying, Homer, maybe we should sit down for a while and have some lemonade. But Homer kept tossing the stick, and Hank kept getting it. So I went up to the pouch and sat in my rocker first.

Homer followed along, and Hank sat by his side alongside the swing. Miss Mary brought some lemonade, and we sipped it slowly, savoring the flavor for a while. Poor Hank was panting, and big drops of water dropped off his long tongue. When the lemonade was nearly gone, Homer suggested we go up to Clyde's and walk the extra mile with him. I didn't quite understand what Homer said, but walking the extra mile was not on my to-do list for this Saturday. I told Homer I still had some things to do and thought I had not better go. Homer asked what I had to do yet. Homer stumped me, and I said I could do those things tomorrow, as that is when I do most things anyway.

Homer, Hank, and I walked down to Homer's Studebaker coupe and climbed in for the ride to Clyde's Chicken Ranch. Homer liked calling it a ranch, and that was okay with me. I wouldn't say Clyde was glad to see us when we arrived. I knew he wasn't happy to see me, and I didn't know if Clyde knew Homer. But he should have, as Homer knows everybody everywhere.

We went up to the house, and Clyde kept us waiting about five minutes longer than he should have. Finally, he approached us and asked what we wanted from him. I wasn't about to start another lousy conversation with Clyde, so I left it all to Homer. This meeting was his idea anyway; it was all under his control. Clyde started the talk in his usual pleasant way and asked what that dog was doing here. He said the dog would scare my chickens, and they won't lay an egg. But Homer was ready for Clyde and told him Hank would not scare his chickens but was here to protect his chickens. Homer told Clyde Hank was a trained Bobcat chaser. I said, really. Homer gave me that say-nothing look.

Clyde said if he could chase away that bobcat and keep him out, he could stay. But what is that going to cost me, Homer? Homer explained that Hank was Meme Mims's dog, and she couldn't keep him any longer and offered to let you have him. Clyde said, really. Homer said he had bought 100 pounds of O'Roy dog food and a water bowl. And Clyde said, really, why? Homer said we do not want to slow down the business because you sell eggs to my brother Herman in Charlotte. So it is a good business for everyone. Miss Meme doesn't have to worry about her dog, Herman doesn't have to worry about not getting his eggs, you don't have to worry about the Bobcats, and I don't have to worry about Tom Lively's hand getting his heart broken. Clyde looked at me and said, "I am sorry, sonny." I tried to smile, and with great surprise, I did. All was mended between us.

As I sat in my spot in the old rocker, moving to and fro, I pondered what Homer meant by walking an extra mile with Clyde. As I sipped on another glass of cool lemonade, the adventure began to take shape in my pondering. That first mile with Clyde was a rough one that left me angry. We sometimes resort to anger without genuinely understanding the whole trouble that the other is having. Instead of finding a solution to Clyde's troubles, it took less effort to be finished with him. I festered the evening away in the throne house. Homer went home that evening and looked to the resources he had to solve the problem. Instead of anger, he showed compassion. That is what we are to do: take that which the Lord provides and use it for His glory. As I pondered further, I came to an amazing hope. Suppose Clyde decided to join our little family at the Church on the Knoll.

Caleb Hodge did, and he is a man with a changed heart. I think that if God can change the heart of a man like Caleb, He can change the heart of anyone. If we go that extra mile with one struggling, we might change their lives to a better world. A world without end, amen. ***"Whoever forces you to go one mile, go with him two."*** (Matthew 5:41)

Saint Agnes of Cork

With the autumn season fast approaching, it has been a quick-paced day here at Tom Lively's feed store. The farm folks have been coming in all day needing this and that in preparing for cooler months that lie shortly ahead. The biggest thing on their list has been baling wire to bail up hay and alfalfa for the winter months to feed the cattle. Then, there are mason jars for the women to can up their vegetables and berries. I have wanted some of Miss Reba's stewed tomatoes or Mother Mary's marmalade preserves throughout the day. Oh yes! There is nothing better than her marmalade resting on top of buttermilk biscuits with sausage links gathered around. Usually, my day at the feed store ends at five, but the folks just kept coming, and now it is six as the last pal of mine gathered his purchases and drove off in the pickup truck. I stopped by the post office to gather up the bills and fret over them, and there in the stack was a letter from Aunt Agnes. I was thinking I was about to have an adventure reading this when my mind jumped back a few months back on another Friday afternoon with the key about to turn the lock on the feed store.

Like every Friday, I began to look forward to a personal day around the little cabin in the meadow. Mother Mary had a long list, but I think I may prioritize the list into a shortlist and spend some time with Spenser along the Greenbrier floating in an old tractor tire. With things put in place and the key in the door, I heard the sound of another pickup truck on the street. Turning around, I saw Johnny Crawford with his grinning face, asking if I had a minute. You know, sometimes we say things we do not mean, as I blurted out, "For you, Johnny, my time is yours."

"Your Aunt Agnes wanted me to stop by and tell you that they have a special service tomorrow evening at Grace Baptist, and you should come." I was amazed that Johnny could say all that and not lose his grin. Before I could answer came salvo two. "Yeah, Robert is coming along with us too. Perhaps you and Aunt Agnes and Pierce could come over to the Kountry Kitchen and have a bit to eat before the service." Now Johnny has unloaded all his guns. Aunt Agnes is a very demanding lady, and if she is inviting me, there would be a price to pay if I didn't go. Robert and my son Pierce are like Johnny and me: best friends and seldom separated. Of course, there's Johnny, who always looks so disappointed when I say no. "Are you suggesting, or is this an invite to the Kitchen?" I asked. "Hey, it's on me, bro." That said, it is a done deal, and my shortlist appears to have grown back to a long list.

Spending time at the Kountry Kitchen with Aunt Agnes, Johnny, Pierce, and Robert was pleasant. Johnny didn't spare much on the meal in the Kitchen either. We didn't order off the menu as Johnny knew what Aunt Agnes' favorite was, and that is what we had. Smoked ham, scallop potatoes, corn on the cob, broccoli smothered in cheese, and pumpkin pie for dessert. The conversation was great, mostly because I didn't have to say much or didn't have the opportunity. Aunt Agnes certainly had the gift to carry the topic. Pierce and Robert were busy window-watching, although I know the boys were watching the girls on the sidewalk. Johnny is usually a listener and feels crafty. I had been drawn out of my cabin for the evening.

Agnes kept talking about a fellow named Brendan McGrath from Ireland. He was the one who was having the service at Grace Baptist this evening. Brendan was a missionary that Grace Baptist helped support, and he had come to let the members know how his ministry was going along. Agnes continued about how she would love to go to Ireland, be a missionary, and see the country's sights. I did get to remind Aunt Agnes that we were Scottish, and she smiled at that. "That's right, and Ireland is our neighbor, and you know the Lord says we are to love our neighbor." Aunt Agnes jabbed back in response. I considered calling that a draw and busied myself working on the pumpkin pie.

When we got to the service, the Church was about half full, and we had no trouble finding a front-row seat. Aunt Agnes remarked how fortunate we were to be close to the podium where we could hear everything said. I just had to reply, "Aunt Agnes, we are in a Baptist Church, and nobody sits in the front seat." If smiles could kill, then I died with Aunt Agnes happy. The service began with nimble fingers dancing across the keys of the piano playing "Onward Christian Soldiers," which I almost remarked was a fitting song for a missionary service but remembered the smile of Aunt Agnes.

After the praise music, Pastor Waylon came out and told us we were in for a special treat this evening as Brendan McGrath, our missionary to Ireland, was here to tell us all what the Lord is doing with his ministry in Ireland. Then Brendan McGrath came and told us all the exciting things happening there in Cork, Ireland. They had a hall for the homeless and discarded of Cork. He told how they would visit the parks and countryside, helping the people clean up their homes and land. But the most exciting was the street ministry in Cork itself. He told how their teams would spend the day going up and down the streets of Cork, sharing the Good News of Jesus Christ. Brendan said that many would rather not be bothered with their interruption on the high end of town, but people were very interested in the low end of town.

He praised that lives were changed no matter where they went, and many made decisions for Jesus. Brendan talked about how this year, they had a band and a rented hall in town that they turned into a club for the town's young people. He said every night, the club was filled with young people who enjoyed the singing and fellowship and listened to the testimonies of what Jesus had done in the lives of others. Increasingly, many would come on Sundays when they had a formal Church service to grow the people in their faith.

As I looked around the sanctuary, the people there seemed interested and sometimes shouted an Amen. It was an amazing evening to hear the mighty works that the Lord was doing in other parts of the world. I felt that he was a man who had answered the call of Matthew 28:19-20 and was not only doing the good work but living an abundant life. There was a special joy about him. It is not the fake joy salesmen have about a product they are trying to sell but the profound joy that comes from within. I was impressed and started scratching around in my pocket, as I knew there would be an offering to give to his ministry.

He closed this by saying the world is busy, and people fill their time in a hurry but never go anywhere. There is a better place, a more incredible plan, and a divine mission leading to Heaven's gates. Jesus said, ***The harvest is plentiful, but the laborers are few; therefore beseech the Lord of the harvest to send out laborers into His harvest.*** (Luke 10:2). As I was clutching a few dollars to offer, Brendan finished with this call. Ladies and gentlemen, if you feel a spiritual tug on your heart, if you want to be a part of something bigger than we are, if you want to find a greater place, and if you want to be a part of a divine mission, then I invite you to join our team. To my shock, Aunt Agnes and Robert got up and went forward and stood with Brendan.

As I was walking Aunt Agnes home after the service, I struggled with how I was to oppose her decision to join Brendan and go to Ireland. Finally, I mustered the courage and said. "Aunt Agnes, you are an eighty-one-year-old lady and have no business going to the mission field. And taking Robert with you, who is just a kid out of High School." Aunt Agnes said Robert was eighteen and old enough to do what he felt he should. With that, I replied, "Roberts of age, but you are..." "What?" Agnes asked. I knew the argument was lost, so I told her I wanted a wonderful evening together.

I read the letter from Aunt Agnes, and I was right; it was an adventure. She and Robert are having the time of their life in Cork, Ireland. It was a town built around a monastery, which fit their call to go there. She spoke of how Robert works at the club, telling all about life here in the "Almost Heaven." Then he shifts to talking about Heaven and how to get there. Aunt Agnes said he is doing fine work for the Lord. Agnes tends to the little children in the hall, telling the Stories of David and Goliath, Samson and Delilah, Moses at the Red Sea, and many others. She has become quite a conversation piece among the other workers, and Brendan has named her Saint Agnes.

As I sit here swaying back and forth in the old rocker on my porch, I find a smile attached to my face for Aunt Agnes, Robert, Brendan, and his team of harvesters. They are having the time of their lives that will live with them throughout eternity. I think we, as people, place our restrictions upon ourselves and miss the true life that we can have. An eighty-one-year-old lady and an eighteen-year-old boy found their life by losing their limitations. It may not be the proper verse of Scripture, but it is the one that flows through my mind. ***For whoever wishes to save his life will lose it; but whoever loses his life for My sake will*** find ***it.*** (Matthew 16:25)

The Rescue of Snuffy Smith

I must say this evening's musings began late yesterday at Lively's Feed Store, Where I work throughout the week. It was near closing, and I was planning my escape from the ever-continuing list of chores Miss Mary wrote during the week. She seems ever inspired with work for me to do as she looks about the little cabin, the children, and the life we share together. This week, the list contained the worst of the worst for me to accomplish. That faded picket fence around the garden needed whitewashing. I like working in the garden, as it is a joy to see the sprouts of seeds planted popping out of the ground and maturing into wonderful things to eat. I wouldn't say I like whitewashing the fence in particular.

I remember the old story that Mark Twain wrote of Tom Sawyer and how he tricked his friends into whitewashing the fence for his Aunt Polly. The trouble for me is that it is hard to trick my peers into such a thing at my age. Perhaps, and I must admit, it would be fitting to whitewash the fence and scratch it off the list. After all, there's a place for me at mealtime, my clothes are washed, and the house is sparkling. Then the door to the feed store opened, and in came Amos Golf. Amos runs the Talcott Dairy and supplies Ballengee with fine dairy products. He still makes home deliveries, except walking up the path to the little cabin, which is a bit far, so we buy our milk at Meaders Market.

Amos unwittingly solved my chore list with a problem of his own. He had to deliver a milk cooler to Alderson and needed my help to make the delivery. Amos said his regular help had to go to Beckley and old Jack was too old. I reminded Amos that I was no spring chicken myself. I said I would do my best wrestling the cooler with him, not to discourage him or lose the opportunity. So the date was set: Amos would pick me up in the morning, and we would ride to Alderson and make the delivery.

Two hours didn't seem like enough time to get out of the whitewashing chore, so I thought I would offer him lunch in Alderson. Alderson is about twenty-three miles out on Highway 20, east of Ballengee. It should only take about forty-five minutes there, a half-hour to deliver, and forty-five minutes back. Better yet, Amos should offer me lunch. Either way, a lucky date would be made to use time.

The ride to Alderson took longer than I expected. Amos' old delivery truck, somewhere over the years, had lost its spunk. It was a '57 International Harvester Metro, scuffed up white paint, and that big milk cooler in the back cabin was slowing down the firing of the pistons. So we spent an hour rolling up and down the hills of Almost Heaven to Alderson. Amos seemed to have much to say, but I could not follow his conversation. He kept talking about his herd of 200 Holstein-Friesian dairy cows. He kept telling me that they were the best milk cattle that God ever created. I couldn't argue with Amos. mostly because I didn't know the difference between cows. My mom had a Jersey cow that she milked, and that seemed enough. Amos kept talking about how many gallons he would get daily, and I thought we were happy to get one gallon.

Finally, we reached Alderson and made our delivery. Getting that milk cooler off the truck and into the store was not bad. Amos took the supervisor job, I was the guide, and the store stock boys did the hard work. So, I got a free ride and, as it turned out, a free lunch at the Alderson New York Style Sandwich Shop. Amos had a ham and cheese on rye while I was the glutton I was, and I had a Rueben with extra corned beef. They also had the best Lemon Ade, and I had two glasses just in case the long, hot trip back made me thirsty. With that, Amos said if I was worried about being thirsty, I could jump into the Greenbrier and float back to Ballengee.

The International rode much faster on the way back without the heavy cooler in the back, but it was a much bumpier ride. I felt like asking Amos if he could miss a pothole now and then, but I decided to enjoy the lemonade instead. I worked for Amos in my younger years, and he can sometimes be a little grumpy when things are not just how he likes them. I spent a summer on his dairy farm running a tractor, going around, and picking up cow pies in the field. It was not the best job I had, but at the time, it provided me a start in spending a little money to impress the girls. After that, I moved on to better things, I thought, and worked at a chicken farm. I was supposed to clean the coops and feed the chickens. Feeding the chickens wasn't bad, but if I thought cow pies were nasty, let me be the first to say chicken specs are much worse. You can walk around a cow pie, but you can't avoid chicken specs getting all over the boots. Mom would make me undress on the back porch, which I didn't like.

As we were both lost in our thoughts, I saw the sign for Pence Springs. I remarked, hey, we are almost home, and Amos said just a couple more hills, and we would be there. We came up behind a deep blue 1953 Plymouth Belvedere Coupe near Talcott. There was something familiar about that car, but I just couldn't put it together. When we went around a steep curve, I nailed it. The chrome trim was missing from the wheel wells, and I knew we were behind Barney Smith. We had a pet name for Barney Smith, and that was Snuffy. Some would call him Barney Google, but Snuffy stuck.

Snuffy was driving a little crazy, and Amos said I think the boy has had a few Falstaff's too many. The longer we were behind Snuffy, the wilder he drove. After a few miles, I told Amos I thought he was getting wilder. It wasn't much further when it began to look a little dangerous as Snuffy was weaving rather severely over the roadway. Amos and I started to think and wonder what we should do and how to stop Snuffy.

Snuffy was the most aggravated person in Ballengee. I can honestly say there is nothing to like about Snuffy. Snuffy had only two sides: sober and aggravated and drunk and aggravated. If one was to speak to Snuffy, and if he was to answer, it would always be a litany of language not even fitting for a sailor. He had a knack for finding the most unimportant things to complain about, and the solution was always to do away with the situation. He was so hateful that he never said anything nice, even about himself. Snuffy was the most miserable person I have ever known, and I felt that one is much better off not being anywhere near him. As we wondered what we should do and remembered the unpleasant times I had crossed his path, the expected happened.

Snuffy missed a curve and went off into the ditch along the side of the roadway. He was lucky we were not up on a hill, as it would have been a long way to the bottom. Amos looked at me and said he didn't think it was bad enough that Snuffy was hurt. Amos said the best thing we could do was go on, and a State Patrol would come by and take care of him with free accommodation. Much to Amos; disapproval, I suggested we go back to ensure he was not hurt and see if we could help him. Amos didn't argue the change in plan, slowed down, and turned the big truck around to go back.

I am not about to repeat what Snuffy said when we walked down the ditch he was in. The rough ride through the ditch sobered him up but did not affect his attitude. At first, Snuffy blamed the whole thing on

Amos and I followed him too closely. Then, it was the state's fault for not broadening the shoulder. Amos offered to ride Snuffy into Ballengee, where he could find help. No, that would not work for Snuffy, as he could not leave a valuable Plymouth Belvedere stranded along the highway for thieves to molest.

Well, we thought we would go and get a chain and pull him out of the ditch, and then he could be on his way. But Snuffy said there was no way we would yank his car around with a chain. Okay, Snuffy Amos said. You look okay and unhurt, so we're going on, and you figure it out for yourself. We both started to walk back to the truck and make our way home. Snuffy reconsidered, and we got a chain and pulled him up to the highway. Then we noticed the flat tire, and Snuffy started ranting that we should buy him a new tire. Amos gave Snuffy that you're out of your mind look.

It turns out that Snuffy had a spare that he knew nothing about, and we put that on the car for him while he supervised with more of his useless chatter. Amos said we would be doing a disservice with that if we let Snuffy drive to Ballengee. I agreed, but my question was, how will we convince Snuffy? Amos, being the manager he is and never taking a no against the right, told Snuffy he would ride in the truck or walk to Ballengee. There has to be a talent to be able to do that, as Snuffy agreed. I thought that was probably the only thing he had ever agreed to. Thankfully, I drove Snuffy's car and followed Amos and Snuffy into Ballengee.

Now, as I drift to and fro in the old rocker, glancing at a picket fence that is in dire need of a whitewashing. The hatefulness and ungratefulness of Snuffy Smith captured me. I couldn't help but try to understand how one could tell Snuffy about God's love for him. I'm unsure I understand how God could love Snuffy, but He does. Perhaps it is not for me to understand because God knows who is better than He. Maybe it is enough to be a good neighbor and let God, who knows, work it out. The question is not whether Snuffy misbehaved but whether Amos and I did what pleased the Lord. As I drift forward and back, I feel that we had. ***And he said, The one who showed mercy toward him. Then Jesus said to him, Go and do the same.*** (Luke 10:37)

<u>Glory to the Hero</u>

Saturday is a day to set aside from the week's labors at Tom Lively's feed store and take in the beauty of the sun's ascent above the eastern mountains that rise about our little community. It is a breezy summer morning here in Ballengee. I find myself slowly rocking back and forth in the old rocker on the log cabin porch, which I call my castle in the majestic hills surrounding the Almost Heaven. As the sun continues to climb to its highest noon perch, I know the temperatures will also rise. The breeze is cool with a bit of crispness, which almost compels me to jump into the chores I have planned for my day.

There are the ever-persistent weeds that spring up in the garden just as soon, it seems, as their ancestors have been removed. If I ever give myself pause from the diligent removal of those weeds from my garden, they would soon take the lead, robbing the nourishment from the rest of the prized vegetables that reside there. The plump red and yellow tomatoes, the stalks of tall golden corn, snap beans, a row of strawberries, and a few mounds of potatoes greatly inspire the supper table and draw the appetite of all.

I know I should be getting up and going right to my chores, as I do not want the day to get away from me the way it did last Saturday. The earlier Saturday was a fine, crisp morning, which started in the old porch rocker. It, too, was a day to be set aside for the chore of garden mending. It, too, fell to a great fault of mine. I can be so easily distracted from my chores to leisure activities, even if it is not an activity that is high on the attraction list of things I like to do, such as fishing. I do not care for fish, I do not care to clean fish, and I'm not particularly eager to go fishing. I reckon it's fair to say that I am not typical of the menfolk here in Ballengee, as the "gone fishing" signs pop everywhere on a Saturday.

I started getting out of the rocker when Homer Massy walked up the path to my cabin. Homer Massy is a man that I truly admire to the fullest extent. He is among the few who think what you hear and see is just what he is. He is a man who never misses an opportunity to bring the Kingdom of God closer to this old world. The Lord must honor Homer as he is always in the right place to show glory to the Heavenly Father. I hope to attain his level of maturity in my life, both in age and stature, like Homer. So far, I have only been racing to catch his age, but then I wonder if I ever will, as he has always managed to stay twenty years ahead of me. There is one thing that Homer and I share: neither of us likes to go fishing. Perhaps we are the only two in Ballengee with no desire for the sport, which is why I was surprised to see Homer coming up the path with only two fishing poles in his hands.

We greeted each other, and Homer sat down on the porch swing as I returned to the rocker. We sat silent for a moment, and then Homer asked if I'd like to go fishing with him down at the Greenbrier. I wouldn't, actually, but I enjoyed Homer's company so much that I said, "Sure." So, I made us some bologna sandwiches, grabbed a couple of apples off the tree, and off we went to the Greenbrier, each carrying a fishing pole. I knew we were about to have an adventure, as neither of us knew how to catch a fish.

We ended up along the banks of the Greenbrier at one of the few places where we knew the water was deep enough for large fish to congregate if that is what fish do in their society. Once settled in, we each grabbed a fishing pole, and it dawned on me that we had no bait. I asked Homer what we would use for bait, and he replied with a question. "Do we want to catch a fish?" I knew I didn't and figured he didn't, so we cast our lines and sat there, taking in the peaceful sounds of a passing river.

One common subject to each of us is talking about the Church. The Church on the Knoll, in particular, was attended by us both. So, we discussed the improvements we would like to accomplish to the Church building and grounds. We discussed some of the victories and trials of other members we knew about. And, of course, we talked about Brother Simms and the messages he gave us on Sunday. Homer spoke about the fascinating subject of the history surrounding the Ballengee community, which always causes my ears to perk up.

All in all, it was a wonderful way to spend a Saturday. We enjoyed the beauty of the nature God had surrounded us. I enjoyed the nature of God in my friend Homer, and it was enjoyable to feel the peace of country life in the Almost Heaven of Ballengee.

The ground rises about fifty feet in a short space from where Homer and I were fishing or just sinking our lines into the drifting waters of The Greenbrier. A young man, maybe late teens to early twenties, jumped off and dove into the river from the top of the rise. The splash of the first dive surprised us, and if there were any fish even thinking about biting a bait-less hook, that now would not happen. Our conversation lightened up as we watched the diver climb back to his perch to dive again. He dove again into the Greenbrier, which was a fantastic dive. It was what I called in my mind a double twister. As he dove into the water, he twisted around three times and did three somersaults simultaneously, diving into the water in perfect form, hands first. Not being an expert diver either, I thought maybe he was practicing for the Olympics. Homer and I watched him dive several times before we returned to our conversation.

We returned to chit-chat about events in Ballengee and were again interrupted by the sound of a hard thud and the horrible splash of a belly flop. Experiences have taught me that this dive of the diver had to hurt. The real scary part of the miss-dive was the diver did not come up after landing in the water. When I realized he was in trouble, I set down the pole and went into the river to fish him out before he drowned. The water of the Greenbrier is clear, and it was no problem finding where the diver was. I grabbed him by the shoulders, brought him to the surface, and managed to bring him to shore.

He was badly choked up from the water he had taken in, so we put him on his stomach, and Homer started pushing some of the water out of his lungs. I took off up the path to the gravel road where the 57 Ford pickup was to get a blanket from behind the seat. I don't know why I did that, but it seemed like it needed to be done for the young man. I returned to Homer and the young man where Homer had him revived, and they talked a little bit together. I wrapped the fellow, whose name Homer told me was Frank, in the blanket. We walked him up to the truck and took him to the Ballengee clinic.

Like always, being with Homer is an adventure about to happen. Things always happen where Homer is, and when Homer, who always takes the initiative, gets involved, the outcome is always for God's glory. I reckon I had better explain that to you as well.

Sunday was another fine day at the Church on the Knoll. Brother John gave us a thoughtful Sunday school lesson on the saving grace of God from Ephesians 2:8. Brother Simms spoke of remembering the defining moments of life. He spoke of our salvation by the cleansing blood of Jesus, Baptism as our testimony of the renewed life that we now have, and the Holy Communion of the Lord's Supper, how they all show us

God has a love for man, the crown of His creation. And that we should share that love with everyone the Lord brings into our path.

Brothers John and Simm's message prompted Homer Massy to stand before our little Church family after the service and testify about our fishing trip experience. Of how Frank had sunk into the waters of the Greenbrier, and I fished him out. Of how we sat there with him on the bank and how the Lord used Homer to lead Frank to the realization that he was a lost sinner in need of God's free gift of salvation, as we never know what lies ahead just a minute away. And the miracle that God performed by saving Frank's soul. It was a moving testimony that only Homer Massy could give in such a miraculous way. As the members of our Church family listened in silent awe to Homer's testimony, the door of the Church opened.

From the back of the Church, a young man named Frank walked forward to the front and stood before the congregation. He came to testify of the greatest hero in his life. In my small-minded way, I thought that I was about to be embarrassed. Frank began to say that all was lost through the scariest moment in his life. He felt a loss that was so deep that there would never be a way to find an escape. Then, as Mister Massey shared the Good News of Jesus Christ, he felt hope as never before. Frank said, "I have come here today to this Church to thank the greatest Hero that has ever been in this world, Jesus Christ." Last Sunday at the Church on the Knoll was, I must say, a defining moment in all our lives there at the gathering.

Now, as I prepare to rise and get the gardening chores done, as much as I need to get caught up on the chores around this old cabin home in the Almost Heaven, it sure would be an excellent day for Homer and me to go fishing for men. The ones from last Saturday and today, I somehow, in the near back of my desires, hope that Homer will come walking up the path with two fishing poles.

Gone Fishing

It has been a hot summer's day here in Ballengee, as the temperatures have climbed up to the '90s, and the fan at the feed store just wasn't enough to bring complete comfort from the heat. I have been rather busy through the morning at Livery's Feed Store. I've been mostly carrying out salt blocks for the herd stock of the farmers in the area. Tommy Thompson needed another water tub for his lower field so the cattle could have a drink. Neil Cunduff called and said he needed some Alfalfa seed he wanted to plant for winter feed. I loaded up the Ford pickup and took the seed to his place along the Greenbrier.

After delivering the seed into Neil's barn, I find comfort in sitting in the Barger Springs Gazebo built around the sulfur spring not far from the banks of the Greenbrier River. I would have liked to visit Neil for a spell, but he was not home, as his sign "Gone Fishing" was hanging on the barn door.

Neil retired several years back as our town constable, and unfortunately, it was an unremarkable event in our history. For over thirty years, Neil watched over our little community here and was more of an arbitrator than a crime investigator. Here in Ballengee, we do not have much criminal activity, as in a town our size is about 2500, everyone knows everyone. Not much goes on that does not funnel down through the reliable channels of local chatter. One might say that our paper, the Ballengee Record, is not the news but a review of life in our little community. Outside of some mischievous youth or one who had one too many at the Back Street Pub, a constable must mostly settle neighbors' disagreements. Over the years, Neil became an expert at finding a justifiable middle ground to resolve the tensions peacefully. If I were to give Neil a title, it would not be constable but a peacemaker.

After Neil retired, he and his wife, Nellie, bought a cottage along the bank of the Greenbrier River. Across from his "Cottage on the Brier," as Neil calls it, is a parcel of cleared land with a slight upward slope that Neil has leased to Angus Miller's farm. Alfalfa and hay are grown for winter feed on this ground, as Angus Miller Jr. is a cattle farmer like his father Angus was. In the 1800s, the White Sulfur Springs Lodge rested on this land. Folks would come from all over to stay there and drink the water from the Barger Spring Gazebo.

Some say the water from the spring holds a therapeutic value for medical benefits, but I could never drink it for the taste and smell remind me of eggs that have long past their prime. Yet many years ago, folks gathered here in hopes of improving their health. Today, the lodge is gone, and what was once a large green lawn of grass became a meadow and now a field for planting winter feed.

I have spent time at Neil's cottage on the Brier, visiting from time to time, as it is a peaceful place to spend time and chat about times now past. From inside the cottage, you can hear the sound of water rushing over the rocks in the shallow riverbed of the Greenbrier. It is a mighty sound that alerts one's senses to the reserved powers of nature while echoing throughout the trees in concert with the leaves dancing in the summer breeze—a large room Inside the cottage, which Neil calls the trophy room. The large ones that did not get away are mounted on one wall. Beautiful largemouth bass, river trout, and one colossal catfish Neil caught by the dam on the Bluestone River hold their position proudly on the wall. As Neil says, many photographs of folks who have passed this way are on another wall. Most of the photographs were taken at the nursing home on the upper side of Ballengee, the Ballengee Atrium. Neil raised my eyebrows when he called the Atrium the fishing hole. Here at Atrium, the elders of our community can no longer manage their independence or whose health now requires constant watch, spend the remainder of their days with their peers.

I have been to the Atrium twice over the years. Once, several years ago, I went with Homer Massy to visit his mother. Homer said you could tell who is new to the Atrium and who has spent some time there. The new residence will often have visits from family and friends. But as time gains its distance, so does the expanse between the visits. It is sad to think that a life of love and devotion is lost in the busyness of the day's endeavor to move further up the ladder of life. True, the Atrium provides activities for its residences; as time takes its toll, many become confined to their rooms. Too often, we say tomorrow we shall visit our loved ones, but tomorrow never comes, and the opportunity becomes lost. Another regret we must bear until our time comes to rest at the Atrium.

The second time I visited the Atrium was last Tuesday night. It was a gala held in honor of Neil and Nellie Cunduff for their faithful commitment to visit the folks at the Atrium. For more years than even his constable position in Ballengee, Neil had been a steady visitor to the Atrium. At first, he and Nellie came at least once a week. Then, several times a week and lately, Neil and Nellie would greet the folks at the Atrium every day. I have always deeply admired Neil and Nellie to the point that I also felt shame for my lack of involvement. Over the years, I remember that Neil would give of his time spent at the Atrium with us each Wednesday at the Church on the Knoll. We heard many stories of trials and victories from the elders lodged at the Atrium, along with the many prayer requests that the folks there had.

Neil once told me that a good fisherman had five essential traits. A good fisherman must be patient and wait for the fish to grab hold of the bait. He must have perseverance and be consistent with his activity. He must have good instincts and be at the right place at the right time. A fisher must remain out of sight as much as possible. A good fisher cannot catch a fish unless he drops a line into the water. It is here today that I now understand what Neil was talking about.

As I sit here at the spring looking into the water I never intend to drink, I realize it is the same attitude we carry throughout our lives. The cup of truth is one we know someday we shall have to drink of, and then the moment comes when we know that time could be just a second away. We don't fear what we know as much as the unknown. For the folks at the Atrium, their moment of truth has come at their loneliest time. It would remain that way for them if not for Neil, who is there fishing with the bait of God's love.

Neil and Nellie spent their time at the Atrium with patients, waiting on the Lord to give His call. They persevered through all the rejection until the spirit was ready to answer His call. They didn't pester the folks but had the good instincts to know when they were prepared to accept Jesus as their personal Savior. Neil and Nellie knew it was the Lord's work and gave God all glory for the salvation of their souls. Neil would say that all he and Nellie did was drop the line in the water. For the folks at the Atrium in the hour of their greatest trial, Neil and Nellie were there to help them find the way. Neil and Nellie are also examples that we all should aspire to, ***Honor your father and your mother, that your days may be prolonged in the land which the LORD your God gives you.*** (Exodus 20:12)

Some folks grab the cross of salvation with both hands and never let go. For them, I find great joy in my heart. Then, some hold to the cross with only one hand and extend the other hand to help others find their way to the saving grace of Jesus. For them, I have the greatest admiration.

On the barn next to the Cottage on the Brier, a sign hangs with "Gone Fishing." Beneath those words, you will also see the inscribed Matt. 4:19. *"Follow Me, and I will make you fishers of men."*

<u>Lily Bridge</u>

I am sitting here sifting through the millions of stars in the late evening sky while sitting on the porch in my old rocker. As I move back and forth in the to and fro of my thoughts, I ponder the extraordinary events of the day here in Ballengee. It is a Thursday evening, and I should be finding my way to bed, as tomorrow is a day filled with Lively's Feed Store duties. But for now, I am content to linger here and extract the rewards of the day's activities. As I watch the stars in the sky twinkling their report to the alleviated glow of the moon's radiance, the thoughts planted long ago and joins together with the experiences that blossomed in the garden of today. I find it a great comfort that subtle heroes of our past have prepared us for the present, and the experiences of the day fortify our steps into the future we have yet to face.

This day began, and now it ends on the porch pondering in my old rocker. Before working at Lively's Feed Store, I treated myself to breakfast at the Kountry Kitchen. I shared a table with Homer Massy, Johnny Crawford, and Caleb Hodge, my fellow members of last evening's gathering at the Church on the Knoll, for our Wednesday Bible Study. Our study and discussion were in John 15:5, where Jesus said he was the vine and we were the branches. ***"I am the vine, and ye are the branches: He that abideth in me, and I in him, the same bringeth forth much fruit: for without me ye can do nothing."*** We each sat there explaining our thoughts on the meaning of the verse in addition to Brother John's lesson. I sat there enjoying the viewpoints of each one's expression and amazed that God must have illuminated each one as we rested through the night.

While amid our theological debate, Rufus Golf came in and sat at the table next to ours. Rufus is generally a steady sort who keeps an even keel and has a calm atmosphere. But today, we could easily see he was in a state of exasperation. Rufus is a sub-contractor who works at the Bluestone Dam, where the Bluestone River joins the Greenbrier River to form the New River. Several years back, it was decided to restructure the dam to produce hydroelectric power for Summers County, Ballengee, and the surrounding areas.

As we turned our attention to Rufus, I asked him why he was so upset. Rufus explained that he hired a new assistant to help wire the electrical panels that control water flow to each turbine in the dam on Monday. Rufus spent Monday with his new assistant, Billy Bob, giving him a tour of the dam and a general project layout. He also gave Billy Bob a blueprint of the dam and the schematic of each electrical panel that needed to be wired. Billy Bob on Tuesday went through the expected problems of the first day on the job but managed to make some progress with Rufus' help. Come Wednesday, Billy Bob did not show much improvement, and Rufus once again ended the day telling Billy Bob to study the blueprints and schematics to accomplish his job's challenges.

Again, today, there was no satisfactory advancement in Billy Bob's performance, and Rufus was constantly being called to help him work through each panel. I waited to hear Rufus finally say he had let Billy Bob go, but that did not happen. As Rufus continued to give his account of Billy Bob, we admired his patience working with Billy Bob. At the end of his story, Rufus says he again tells Billy Bob to continue studying blueprints and schematics.

Before we ended our breakfast meeting, I asked Rufus if he thought Billy Bob would ever catch on. Rufus said he felt Billy Bob was earnest enough but wasn't placing the needed information in his mind to draw upon it when each situation developed in the dam. With that being the closing thought, we bid farewell and ventured to face another wonderful day here in Ballengee.

The rest of my day was spent at my place of duty at Lively's Feed Store. As the chores of the day wore on, I began to look forward to our evening plans, which were to be spent with Martha Lily, one of those mighty people who helped guide me in the days of my youth. We spent our time together, Miss Lily, Brother Simms, Mother Mary, and myself, playing Bridge and discussing our past adventures in Almost Heaven.

Miss Lily was my Sunday school teacher in those long-ago years of my youth. I remember many Sunday school lessons she taught at James Street Presbyterian Church. But as we all sat together playing Bridge, reminiscing over the times gone by, one of those old chapters from Sunday school again opened up, requiring a review of thoughts once resolved. It amazes me that as we travel through life, many events will come around again as either a confirmation or evaluation to assure and quiz us of our track.

Miss Lily would give us a Bible verse to memorize and learn each Sunday. During the week, we were to think about our assigned verse and then tell her and the rest of the class what that verse meant. One Sunday, she assigned the verse John 1:1 to me. ***"In the beginning was the Word, and the Word was with God, and the Word was God."*** (KJV) I spent the first part of the week memorizing the verse, and as I recited the verse each time, more thoughts of what it meant came to my mind. As we made our way to church the following Sunday, I had a lot to say about John 1:1. I sat in Sunday school class anxiously, forcing patience for my turn to speak. I felt that if I didn't get it out soon, I would forget it. My turn finally arrived, and I explained that the verse meant God's word in the beginning, which was the Bible. Because the Bible says we have to tell the truth, God had to keep his word, and because God kept His word, He became His word.

Martha Lily said that was a very good explanation. She said that a man was only as good as his word when he was growing up. If we put God's word in our hearts, our words will always be true. Miss Lily said we put God's word into our hearts by attending Sunday school every week and learning a new Bible verse. By putting God's word into our hearts, we would have them guide us through each day and encourage us to live good lives and not be bad.

I was sitting there contemplating the odds of, consistently with 13 cards dealt in each hand of Bridge, why I had failed to come up with more than one face card. Brother Simms brought up the subject of John 1:1. Miss Lily immediately asked me if I was still placing God's word in my heart. Of course, I answered with the obvious reflection of a quilt on my face that I wasn't. I was relying on the fact that each Sunday afternoon, in part, was spent pondering the lesson given by Brother John each Sunday at the Church on the Knoll. Brother Simms continued his conversation with John 1:1, relieving me of further testing my shallow declaration.

As I continued to collect faceless cards dealt into my hand, Brother Simms said that John's gospel stated in this first verse of his gospel that Jesus was the full revelation of God's Word. Jesus did not come only to tell us what God was like but to show us what God is. Jesus did this not only by His faithful relationship with God but also by showing that He was God in man's flesh. Then, through Jesus, we can come to know God fully. Miss Lily agreed that there was a great power to be found in Brother Simm's interpretation. She also said that by placing our trust in

Jesus' direction, we could have a spiritual abundance filled with victory over the pitfalls of life.

We continued to play a few more hands of Bridge while I feasted on Miss Lily's blueberry cornbread cupcakes. As the early evening moved on to a time long enough for a night out, Mother Mary pointed out that it was nearly past my bedtime. After all these years, much longer than I would admit, I still find that I'll be under the direction of a caring soul to tell me I am past my time for bed. Mother Mary and I thanked Miss Lily for her gracious hospitality, bid our farewell to Brother Simms, and began our journey together to the cabin in the meadow.

With the wind flowing through the leaves, it sounds distant applause to the glorious day the Lord had given us all here in Ballengee. Though I am far past the hour of retreat, I just cannot let go of the marvel of this day's adventure. With each promise, I shall stand to go inside on every forward movement of the rocker. Still, I explore the truth of the power of God's word. His word was in the beginning, and all came after by the power of God's word. The word was with God, and He revealed His plan for humanity through the life of His Son, Jesus. The word of God through Jesus is integrated into the will of God the Father. The example of Jesus' life in every word He spoke and every action of His life here was in complete obedience to the will of the Father. Jesus is the measure that our lives must aspire to become. Living a perfect life as Jesus did is an impossible accomplishment for us, but through His gracious sacrifice, we can be seen as pure in the Father's eyes. Jesus is the living word of God. By abiding in His Spirit, which dwells within us, we can achieve an abundant Christ-like life.

As I rock back through the day's events, I wonder why Billy Bob could not see that his study of the blueprints and schematics would bring him success in his efforts at the dam. I marvel at Rufus's patience and unwavering desire to help Billy Bob become an acceptable employee. In the days of my youth, Martha Lily showed me the bridge to the truth and victory in life. It is very simple for us to claim the victory in the battle that has already been won. By following the master carpenter and placing His blueprint for our lives in our hearts, we can defeat the devil, as Jesus did with the word of God. With that last forward rock in my old rocker, I retire to my room in peace.

Upon the Rocks

It was a snappy Saturday here in Ballengee. Yes, this time of year is my favorite time. Nature has put on her marvelous display of color. The wind is crispy, and I can now wear my jacket. I have always loved jacket weather. Perhaps it has always provided the extra security of hiding those love handles or that ever-present padding around the middle I have across the top of my belt.

Nonetheless, I enjoy the warmth of a jacket. You can do things with a jacket that you can't do with a shirt. Wear your favorite lapel pin or sew a football patch on your jacket. I like the safety pin given to me by a previous employer for years of safe driving. Most of all, my West Virginia state patch and General Lee's Battle flag are sown above the pockets. I can't pin those on a shirt without looking weird, but it looks fine on a jacket.

The sun shone full this morning here in Ballengee, and amid the cool air, its warmth feels good. It's the morning when the weekly trek to Crawford's Kountry Kitchen is brisk and good for the old Thumper in the chest. I've known John Crawford ever since, but I never thought he would open a restaurant in beautiful downtown Ballengee. I thought he'd grow up like most of us and work the land for a living.

Most of them are farmers who work on the land of their families. But John picked up the trade from his mother's great cooking talent. If you ever get to Ballengee, stop at Crawford's Kountry Kitchen and experience the culinary delights there. If you ever long for the fabulous meals that Grandma used to make every Thanksgiving, then Crawford's is the place to go anytime. I remember one time I was laid out for a whole afternoon after being slapped in the mouth by a rack of ribs. It was a long time before my taste buds could again be satisfied.

John has done a marvelous job with the decor of his Kountry Kitchen. It is a setting that makes one feel they are in an old farmhouse kitchen. In most restaurants, you can't see the kitchen or the folks preparing the food, but at the Kountry Kitchen, this is not true. There is no divide between the kitchen and the restaurant; there is just a counter where one can sit if he wishes to. The old wood stove is now fixed with gas burners beneath the iron plates. The counters are made of linoleum, and there is a square solid oak table with a thick oak slab for a top. The cooking pans are cast iron, and the pots are porcelain. Much the same as most of us when growing up on the farm. Around the eating area and above the booths are antiques, each bringing back memories of younger days. The walls are of dark siding set off by the oak wood booths with red plastic cushions, which look and feel like leather. The chairs and tables in the middle of the room look much like the old family dining tables of long ago. They are made of cherry wood and have the same red plastic cushions as the booths. Along the walls are old photographs of earlier days in the Ballengee area and portraits of citizens from the long past. So often, folks come in to eat in the company of past relatives, and I have even seen some saying to them a hello or goodbye, or maybe just a comment to say how they are doing.

Every Saturday, the older fellows gather in the corner booth beneath the portrait of Ballengee's founding father, Robert Ballengee, to discuss the whims and ways of life in this old world. I remember when I was a kid, and I would like to think it wasn't that long ago. I wanted to be older, and now that I am, I sometimes wish I were younger. That desire has recently passed, and I find myself more and more satisfied with my present age. I have always regarded my elders as not older people but those of greater wisdom and experience. Listening to their stories of yesteryears is a most favored and fascinating pastime for me at the Kountry Kitchen. There is much to learn from the episodes of those who have traveled the road before. So I joined the old fellows, who are not so older now, at Crawford's for the conference and enjoyment of sharing, learning, and expounding points of view.

This week, Nolan Richardson came down from his homestead of Eagle's Perch to enjoy the low landers, as he likes to say. He comes down to learn what is happening in the world but usually becomes the prominent director of the conversation. Nolan's young age of 97 offers a broad range of experiences and no loss of contribution to the general forum. It is always a treat when Nolan is at Crawford's, and today was no exception. Nolan has been around long enough now that he needs never make excuses, as he knows as much about everyone and their families as any. I have been amazed to learn things about my ancestry from Nolan that I didn't know and, of course, knowing what happened in familiar places before you discovered them is always interesting. A chat with Nolan can bring Ballengee's history to life as if it were all in the present. With Nolan around today and all those yesterdays, it has become one great living moment.

This Saturday, Nolan and Tommy Thompson strongly discussed who had the best farmland at Crawford's. Tommy Thompson, probably the nearest peer to Nolan, has always made it known how hard life has been in Ballengee. "It wasn't always as easy as it is for you younger ones," Tommy would always say. It is a statement always cued for a story about the wildlife in pre-historic Ballengee. But Nolan responded by saying it doesn't matter where you plot, but how you plot. That sparked an exchange of opposing attitudes, which the rest of us drank along with our coffee and donuts.

The discourse started, I think, over who between them had the most rocks in the soil of their farms. Before any accurate accounting could be done, Homer Massy inserted that the land here was filled with rocks everywhere. Everyone agreed and nodded that rocky soil was a problem that all here at Ballengee had to deal with. We were about to move on, but Tommy would not let that pass, exempting the uniqueness of his land.

"Back when I came here, I had to remove the rocks from the soil with nothing more than a shovel, pick, mule, wagon, and a strong back," Tommy went on. "I worked from sunup to sundown for years clearing the land. I took all those rocks and built the stone fence around my farm you see today."

That is true. I have been to Tommy's farm, and the stone fence stretches for miles all around the boundary of his farm. When I was a kid romping about, I remember seeing Thompson's stone fence and thought it was much like the Great Wall of China. Through the years, moss and ivy have grown on the stone fence, and a lot of that ivy is poison ivy. I climbed over Thompson's stone fence once and suffered for it too.

Well, that is a good thing, I Suppose," Nolan responded, "but you drag them off to the end of your property and pile them there for a hurtle to your neighbors. I collected the rocks and built my house, barn, cellar, and chicken coop, silo, and well with them. Every building on my farm is built from the rocks found on my farm. I am still building from them today."

Our Sunday school class leader, Brother John, said observing how people deal with their problems was interesting. "One builds their home while the other builds a wall. Now, isn't that certainly something to ponder?"

Ponder we did, all of us, until it was near lunchtime, and we all had to go on about our business on this lovely Autumn Saturday. But I don't think we all caught Brother John's meaning in his observation. However, the determination between Nolan and Tommy was that Nolan was thankful for using all those rocks, while Tommy would have been much happier without them.

If Saturday had been a beautiful day, Sunday surpassed it. The warm sun filled the hills and valleys, casting contrasting shadows across the land. The leaves on the trees, now filled with stark colors of red, yellow, and shades of orange, slowly broke loose from their branches and danced in the breeze as they drifted to the ground. There, they lay upon the browning grass and rested in their beauty as if placed by the loving guidance of God Himself. I gingerly walked to the Church by the Greenbrier to give special thanks, as this was the Sunday before Thanksgiving. What better than to provide the Lord with special thanks for the blessings of His bounty and Grace?

After my traditional pondering and quiet time at the brook, I went into the Church and took my place in the rear, waiting for Brother John's Sunday school Bible Class to begin. Even then, his unexplored muse about Nolan and Tommy from the day before remained in my thoughts. Soon, all were seated, and Brother John began his lesson.

After an opening prayer, Brother John opened his bible and read the following passage; ***"As ye have therefore received Christ Jesus the Lord, so walk ye in him: Rooted and built up in him, and established in the faith, as ye have been taught, abounding therein with Thanksgiving.***

Continue in prayer, and watch in the same with Thanksgiving." (Col. 2:7; 4:2). He then began his lesson for this Thanksgiving Sunday.

"The other day, I listened to a conversation between two men about rocks. We all have rocks in our lives and deal with them differently. When I think about rocks and farmland, I see them as obstacles in the path of a good harvest. The rocks must be removed for the earth to produce a good crop. In order for us to live a good life, our rocks must also be removed from our lives."

"One of the two had gathered the rocks and placed them in a circle about him. There they rested, and moss, weed, and poison ivy flourished upon them. No matter which direction he turned, he faced the wall of rocks filled with weed and poison. How many of us do this in our lives? Take our trials and tribulations and place ourselves within the center of them. No matter how we turn, we must face the hardships in our lives. I suspect this man has grown bitter over the years, filled with regret that now he has walled himself in with his problems. What then is his escape, but to face all that he has put around him in his time? How many of us on the Day of Judgment shall first and finally be faced with what we have stored about us? What shall our answer be upon judgment when asked to give an account? I suspect some to say, "Lord, all this trouble came into my life, and I was overwhelmed and knew not what to do." What shall the Lord say? What shall the Lord say that He has not already said in His Word? Why, I ask, do we allow these natural trappings of the earth to overcome us when we have the power to move mountains in His name?"

"The other of the two built his home with the rocks found on his farmland. He took the troubles in his life and employed them to better his life. He used them for profit rather than tossing them about or becoming encircled by his problems. In his later years, his life problems are not burdens of the past but trophies of the future. Laurels that he now can rest upon. He is not bitter nor filled with contempt but proud of his accomplishment. On the day of new trials, he is better equipped to weather the storms that surely shall come."

"I am caused now to think of Job, and that man was perfect and upright, and one that feared God, and eschewed evil. Yet, despite his righteousness, great adversity came into his life. Far greater than that which has come into ours. In the beginning, Job had it all and then lost it all. He lost his possessions, his family, and his health. Yet through it, Job never lost his faith, and he endured. In the end, he was blessed even more than he had been before. I think Job must have been quite a fellow in his day as he certainly caused a stir in Heaven. (Job 1:8-12 KJV) *"and the LORD said unto Satan, Hast thou considered my servant Job, that there is none like him in the earth, a perfect and an upright man, one that feareth God, and escheweth evil? Then Satan answered the LORD, and said, doth Job fear God for naught? Hast not thou made a hedge about him, and about his house, and about all that he hath on every side? Thou hast blessed the work of his hands, and his substance is increased in the land. But put forth thine hand now, and touch all that he hath, and he will curse thee to thy face. And the LORD said unto Satan, Behold, all that he hath is in thy power; only upon himself put not forth thine hand. So Satan went forth from the presence of the LORD."*

"Even a man as great in the Lord as Job has tribulation in his life. Then so shall we, as Satan, constantly going to and fro in the earth and walking up and down in it. He, too, is testing our faith, trying to shake us away from the path and the Will of God. We then must deal with these situations that will and shall come into our lives, and how we do that will affect the outcome of the next. I heard an interesting comment: it's not where your plot is in life but how you plot your life. It is true, and we must bury our foundation in the Word of God. When the tempter comes, when the trials of life come, we shall know what God has planned for us."

"My point, this lovely Thanksgiving Sunday, is the old adage that a little rain must fall into each life. Bad times will come upon us, and how we handle them is more important than the fact that we have the trial in the first place. I think God oversees this and uses these hard times to build our faith, demonstrate his love and power, and prepare us for greater challenges to glorify His name."

This life here is all about our faith and our baptism of fire in which we prove our desire to be righteous. We quickly say thanks for the good things, yet we also complain about the bad. Yet, the reward for overcoming our life's trials is the good we can find within ourselves. Jesus said (Mark 8:34 KJV), ***"Whosoever will come after me, let him deny himself, and take up his cross, and follow me."*** We are not promised a perfect life but an abundant life in the Lord. (Mat 5:11-12 KJV ***"Blessed are ye, when men shall revile you, and persecute you, and shall say all manner of evil against you falsely, for my sake. Rejoice, and be exceeding glad: for great is your reward in heaven."***

"Then should be thankful not only for the many blessings God has showered upon us but also for the rocks found within our soil. These rocks build our strength and prepare us for the future challenges we must face. This year, as we celebrate our thankfulness for the blessings we have received throughout the year, let us also remember the trials we faced to receive these rewards. Not only do they strengthen us, but allow us also to demonstrate our love for Him, Jesus the Lord and Master of our lives." Brother John closed with a prayer.

I went home that Sunday with a better attitude towards the problems in my life. There have now been challenges with which I can better myself with the great opportunities to demonstrate the power of God's providence. To endure and overcome in the power of His Spirit is tremendous in our witness for Him. After all, just that little tab of faith we showed initially can only grow when tested. What is faith without proof? James wrote in the second chapter that faith without works is dead. Think about that. If we have an active faith, we should be able to leap upon the rocks for Jesus.

A Watch and Follow Parade

Spring is now unfolding here in Ballengee, and the renewing of nature is lifting the spirit. The buds upon the trees are bursting into light green leaves. Dandelions are now roaring across the lawns of fresh green grass. The flower beds are a rainbow of color, as the flowers dance in the springtime breeze here in the Appalachian Mountains of the "Almost Heaven." The newness of color returning to the former brown and gray landscape is a new cleanness and purity. It's holding all the innocence and boldness of youth born into a world that hungers for rebirth. Yes, this perhaps is my favorite time of the year. Nature is at her best, and all of God's handiwork is a beauty.

It is Easter time, and Ballengee folks work hard each year to have a dazzling Easter Parade. I admit that it is not as spectacular as the one down Fifth Avenue in the big city, but it holds its special meaning for us. As in most small towns across America, the folks of Ballengee are but an essential extension of the American family. As we like to say, most here know most here, so the Easter Parade is more than a city event; it is a family event. The efforts put into the Easter Parade are meaningful, as we know the craftsman and the craft. Like the Christmas season and all its declarations, work has a certain competitiveness. Each church has a float depicting a religious theme of the Easter season. Saint Joseph's Catholic has a High Priest standing over his flock of perisher offering a blessing. The First Methodist Church follows with its members waving Palm branches towards the crowd along the street. James Street Presbyterian then comes along with their choir, singing Hallelujah.

Grace Baptist Church has a figure of Jesus sitting on a donkey with His Disciples attending Him, and the Church of the Knoll follows behind with the stone rolled away from the empty tomb of Joseph of Arimathea. For the secular of Ballengee, there is a float with the Easter Bunny throwing out candy to the children.

The most inspiring floats are those built by the farming community. I like the touch of floats pulled by mules rather than gas-powered vehicles, although the farm tractor is a fascinating creature in itself. We are treated to the Ballengee High School band and the Firehouse band. Several church choirs perform some of the best vocal music to be heard in the valley. There are also contributions from neighboring communities as well. But I have always felt there is still nothing better than homegrown.

Our Easter Parade is led by the Grand Marshall, who usually is the Mayor. Bobby Ballengee was the reigning Mayor at the time. Bobby is the great-great-grandson of Robert Ballengee, the founder. The Easter Parade begins with the wailing sirens of the police car and fire engine at the head of the procession. The Grand Marshall will ride on top of the fire engine, smiling and waving to us, his loyal subjects. Politicians are always running for the next term. Some Easter Parades you stand and watch, and others you travel with. I suppose this depends upon the size, but in Ballengee, we do both. We stand as the Easter Parade passes and then fall behind and become a part of it. The Easter Parade slowly moves down Arrington Street on past Maxwell to Logan's Park.

There, it ends, and the children have an Easter egg hunt followed by a devotional each church participates in. It is a moving end to this moving event on our calendar.

Bobby Ballengee is quite an elderly fellow now but a tremendous inspiration to us all. He has been the Grand Marshall of the Easter Parade for the second time. The first time was a few decades ago, long before Bobby thought about politics. Though I am not sure he ever did think about politics. Come to think of it, he never ran for mayor; we just appointed him. Bobby Ballengee's previous Grand Marshall Privilege in 76 had a moving story and motivation behind it. It is a story that began in 69 in a faraway, distant land that most of us only heard of and never understood. Seeing Mayor Bobby Ballengee as the Grand Marshall brings back those moments of long ago to my mind as fresh as the new colors all about us here in Ballengee.

I know a story from when I was there in that distant land of Vietnam, and Bobby Ballengee's son Olin was my friend then. We had grown up together, and besides Johnny Crawford, Olin was about as close a friend as one could have. Olin and I joined the army together on the buddy plan and went through boot together. We parted after boot but landed together two months later in South Vietnam and met at the landing strip in Cam Ranh Bay. From there, Olin and I went separate paths. Olin was infantry, and I was a truck driver. I was assigned to a light equipment combat engineer company and sent north to Bon Son.

We met up later in the tenth month of our tour. I was stationed in Plaque, where we were building a hard surface road. Olin was stationed about twenty miles away at a firebase named Weight Davis. He was in the recon platoon and kept an eye on the neighborhood. At Weight Davis, there also was a rock quarry, and we would convoy out in our dump trucks and pick up gravel. While waiting for my load and the convoy to form for the journey back, Olin and I would visit. As time passed, Olin kept mentioning how the neighborhood there was getting crowded. It made sense to me. The V. C. didn't need a firebase out there in the country and certainly one with a rock quarry. The army moved by air and road, and that rock quarry built airstrips and roads.

I knew things were getting hot out there when the security for our convoys was beefed up. We no longer traveled in a group but were accompanied by gun trucks. We assembled to start our convoy one morning, but it was called off, and we were relieved from the day's duty. The news came that Weight Dawis was overrun, and only a few had managed to get out. Olin was listed as Missing in Action and presumed dead. Weight Davis was destroyed and never was reclaimed by our forces.

Not long after I returned home to Ballengee, Bobby Ballengee visited. Bobby wanted to confirm that no one had seen Olin die or that a body was not recovered. I was very uncomfortable in our conversation, as I could not give Bobby any good news. I was there, but not when the base was overrun. I had seen Olin almost every day but not on that last day. I could only tell Bobby about the times we shared at Weight Davis. By the end of our conversation, I was amazed at the hope that Bobby had. His hope and belief were that Olin was not dead and that someday he would return home.

Bobby Ballengee committed himself to getting the whole of the U. S. Military in Southeast Asia to scour the country and find his son Olin. He went on petition drives, hounded Senators, wrote numerous letters to the President, and spoke at all the political functions he could. Bobby never once gave up this mission, nor did he tire of it. Finding his son Olin became his passion and reason for all he did. Many would come to Bobby and say he should accept the reality that Olin had given his life in defense of his compatriots. Many would tell Bobby that this campaign of his would be his death. Even I knew that this was not completely true. I believed Olin to be lost, but Bobby's campaign was the cause of his life. Bobby never gave an inch, and each discouraging word, challenge, and defeat only strengthened his Hope that he would see Olin again someday.

The conflict with Vietnam ended for the United States. Not long after, it became known that Olin was not MIA but a Prisoner of War. Soon, he would be released and return home. In late March of 76, Olin returned to Ballengee, and the town gave him a Hero's Welcome. On the Saturday following Good Friday, Bobby and his son Olin rode on top of the fire engine as the Grand Marshals of the Easter Parade. It was, as I shall never forget, the grandest of all Easter Parades in Ballengee.

Parades have a way of capturing the emotions of those who watch them. Even a lousy Parade can cause a tear to flow when the band passes by— raising our nation's flag jerks at the works of my emotions.

I wonder what the participants of that Easter Parade in Jerusalem felt on that first Good Friday. I'm sure most were caught up in the event's excitement and curiosity, some filled with skepticism, others feeling that justice was being served, some relieved that a threat was passing. I am sure that many there were in great fear and distress. Some who held a great belief in the Grand Marshall of that Easter Parade were having that belief tested. They believed their King, Jesus, who would rule in great power, was now being put to death. Jesus, the Son of God, submitted and powerless in His final moments of life. They, who traveled with, spoke with, and for, professed Him to be who He was; would they also follow in His fate? Would the Jews seek them out and destroy them also? What are their beliefs now? Would their passion also be put to an end? I imagine that some of them were tested to the extreme of their being. This Easter Parade, too, was a watch-and-follow parade. Its path ended at Calvary, where creation put the Creator to death. What sorrow and distress many must have felt as the jubilant crowds mocked, spat, and crucified their Lord and Master.

I thought about that Easter Parade years ago when Jesus was the Grand Marshall. I learned something, or should I better say, I realized the truth. That Hope and Faith are born in the greatest hour of distress. That is our greatest sorrow, and we can find our greatest joy. When we truly desire what we cannot see, our faith empowers us to act.

Bobby never once gave up his hope that Olin would return. Each time that hope was challenged, his hope was strengthened, and his faith grew stronger. If Bobby had not Hoped and acted upon, Faith Olin would have come home to find his tombstone. Our Hope is in the resurrection of God's Son, Jesus, and His return is soon to come. If our Father in Heaven had not raised His Son from the dead, then when we returned home, we too would find our tomb. We have not seen Him yet; we know the truth and, therefore, have Faith. Into every lifetime, sorrow and distress shall come. In these times, we have the opportunity to strengthen our faith and renew our hope. Our faith empowers our hope that we will be in a great Easter parade someday. That resurrected Easter Parade in the clouds with our Risen Lord and Master Jesus Christ. It, too, will be a watch-and-follow Easter Parade.

Get the Connection

Sitting here along the banks of the Greenbrier River, just beneath the presence of the Church on the Knoll, I find myself at my sport, pondering. It is a question that must be answered within the corridors of my memory of the week passed before it drifts into the file cabinet that sometimes opens without reason. It is a bright Sunday morning, in which I enjoyed a wonderful worship service with the Lord and our Church family. The message of Brother Simms was a conclusive word that gave a case for the review of the week past. As I gaze at the swirling water that waves over the sunken rocks resting beneath, I pay particular attention to the one that protrudes above the waterline. The water rushes to the top and forms a mist as it returns to the river's flow. Somewhere in the mist, I see the hint of a rainbow, reminding the promise of God that all things will work for good to those who love Him. I take comfort in this as even now, I am learning the lesson of the moment.

My usual activities of the week carry me not far from the cabin in the meadow, Tom Lively's feed store, and once now and then, a reward trip to Betty Mae's Taste Freeze for a highly decorated Banana Split. This week was exceptional as I was afforded an adventure to Capitol City with Newt Harper, the editor of the Ballengee Record. Newt had an appointment with Governor Bob Timberlake to discuss the opportunity for hydroelectric power to be produced from the dam. So early Wednesday morning, even before the roosters crowed their early morning wakeup call, Newt and I were on our way. The trip itself was an exciting respite from the rut that I so easily had become accustomed to in Ballengee. It was good to get away from the shelter of the comfort zone and see the beauty that lay just beyond the well-traveled paths of home.

We climbed up Jumping Branch on the narrow mountain road to the broad road that led to the seat of power for our great state in West Virginia. With the ear-popping twisting and winding up the mountains and drifting down into the valleys, the wonders of the birthing sun and the fading shadows dancing across with each curve was a marvelous view to take in. Then, once on the broad road, Newt let all six cylinders of his Ford Galaxy pump enough power to race through the rolling hills of the high country. When we dropped down into the Kanawha Valley, we curved along the banks of the still Kanawha River until the sight of the tall buildings of Capitol City were shown in the quick glimpses of the horizon. I had truly enjoyed this ride so far, but now, in the crowded confusion of the city, I was out of my peaceful demure and found myself ready to rest in a relatively less crowded place. I was glad when we parked several blocks from the Governor's Mansion and were prepared for the stroll to his office. I soon learned that strolling was not appreciated in the city as everyone passed quickly, and I felt like I was in their way. Newt was in advance, so I had to pick up my pace or be left in the smog of the mid-morning air from all the traffic horning their way through the streets.

Newt visited with the Governor, which left me with nothing much but time, so I went and sat on a bench alongside the road. I sat there a while, taking in the sight of all the city activity, until a bus stopped and opened the door. The driver sat there impatiently, looking at me. I didn't know what to do, so I grinned and waved at him. He returned a sneer, closed the door, and drove down the street. Thinking that maybe I was in a no-sitting zone, I looked across the street to see a Valley Belle soda shop.

It was near lunchtime, so I crossed the busy street to visit the Belle. Once inside, I looked at the wall of pictures depicting the items they offered, and the sight of a huge Banana Split captured my eyes. It looked very inviting, but I settled on a hamburger and fries with cherry cola. It was good enough and filling, but I must admit, not near the goodness of those I have enjoyed at the Kountry Kitchen back home. The cherry cola was something I would have to tell Johnny about, and I hope he adds it to his menu. It was rather shocking when I paid the bill and had to spend .75 cents for lunch. Wow! It is a big city with significant sights and is expensive.

I spent most of my time wandering the streets and being amazed at the sights you would never see in a small town. When I returned to the Governor's Mansion, I noticed a Gazebo and bought a newspaper, another .20 investment, and sat down to read the history of the news. I read much of the newspaper and was amused by Dagwood and Snuffy Smith when Newt tapped me on the shoulder. Newt said his meeting with the Governor went well, but it wasn't a yes or no conclusion. It was more of a "we will give it some time to ferment" type of conversation, ending with we will be in touch.

Newt and I walked back to his car together, only to find that it would not start. I am always amazed at how things can break when they are idle. Newt lifted the hood, and we stood together looking into the compartment, searching through our lack of understanding of how things inside worked. Newt checked the oil, water, and other fluids while I jiggled all the wires I could find. I don't think we accomplished anything, but it started right up when we got back in the car. Of course, I said it was just a loose wire, and Newt noted the cap on the radiator was loose. Either way, the motor was humming so off on our return trip, giving the matter no more thought.

We had almost forgotten the difficulty of the unwilling engine till we left the flatness of the valley and started to climb back into the hills. There was a vibration throughout the car, and I think it was only running on four of the six cylinders. Not knowing any better, we kept plodding along each hill, giving the Ford more of a challenge until it finally stopped running. Lifting the hood again, Newt and I exchanged places, and I checked the fluids, and he jiggled the wires. Neither of us is mechanically minded. We were hoping against hope that one of us would do something that would fix the problem. We fiddled around and got back into the car, and it started right back up. Off we went, wondering what next was to happen.

The rest of the ride on the broad road wasn't too bad. It was a little shaky going up, but coasting down was okay. We both knew without saying that when we got to the narrow road going down through Jumping Branch, it would not be a good ride for us. We thought we should be smarter about this and stopped at a service station once we got off the broad road.

When we pulled into the service station, a tall, greasy man approached us with Bob's on his shirt. "What can I do for you?" Said he. Newt explained the situation, and we popped the car's hood, and Bob looked around for a while. Newt stayed close to the front of the car while I sat inside, looking around all the places money might be hiding. I wished I had not spent the .95 cents as we might now require it. As I was making another check beneath the mats, I heard Bob shout, "Bingo!" I should have known that Newt, who had connections with the Governor, would also have a little nest egg in his pockets to pay Bob with. With Bob paid off, we went down the narrow road to Ballengee.

The Ford Galaxy was running as great as it ran before it broke parked back in Capitol City, which made the trip more enjoyable. I asked

Newt what Bob had done to make the repairs. Newt explained that the number four-cylinder wire to the distributor cap was badly corroded. Bob removed the wire and cleaned the area with baking soda, removing all the corrosion. Bob also replaced the four and five because they both appeared to have cracks that might cause a bad connection. Newt also said that Bob replaced the distributor cap because the four and six positions had dysfunctional taps and would cause performance loss. Bob had done all this work for the amazingly low price of 1.75 and said that if it wasn't right, make the thirty-mile trip back, and he would give it another shot. I had no idea what Newt was discussing, so I asked, "What was wrong with the car?" "It had lost its connection." Replied Newt.

Now, I find myself sitting here along the banks of the Greenbrier, wondering how Brother Simms knew I had not understood the events of our adventure to Capitol City. As I have said before, Brother Simms is not a dynamic speaker. Still, his value in delivering the Word is that it comes from his heart. Maybe it is not that Brother Simms is a prophet but that the Good Lord was helping me to understand what I had not understood. Perhaps it was just because I hadn't gotten the point of this past week's adventure. Now and then, our loving Lord has to turn on the light for us and then pray that we leave it on.

Brother Simms taught out of Colossians this week, and as always, it was just the right message. His message came from Colossians 2:19. ***Holding fast to the head, from whom the entire body, being supplied and held together by the joints and ligaments, grows with a growth which is from God.*** As we go through life, we are traveling up and down through the hills and valleys of life; if we are right, the up can be handed as well as the down. Sometimes, the up is good, the down is bad, and vice versa. But if all our cylinders are hitting, we can also handle each circumstance.

The Cylinders are love, as God is love. God gives us His love, and by it, we learn to be truly concerned for the spiritual welfare of all we meet. We are to love our neighbors as we love ourselves. In the economy of this world, everyone is our neighbor. We have the commission to tell the gospel story of Jesus Christ so that everyone can come to a saving knowledge of Jesus. If we have love, we can express our love by trusting His Word and by our faith in acting on His Word. Jesus said that if you love me, then you will keep my commandments. It is faith to trust Him and act upon His Word. By our love and faith, we find hope. It is not the hope we find in the world that is not much more than a wish or fantasy, and it is hope found in the promises of God. The cylinders that we go on is, ***But now faith, hope, love, abide these three; but the greatest of these is love.*** (1 Corinthians 13:13)

What if one of these cylinders miss-fires? There would be a loss of our power available to us in the Holy Spirit. What has happened to cause this loss? It is the same as what happened to Newt, me, and his automobile. The corrosion of sin had blocked the connection. Our life is in Christ, and if we are to live abundantly, we must be connected to the source, Jesus Christ. Sin in our life distorts that connection; it weakens the fellowship. Did not disobedience distort the harmony between our parents and us? Disobedience also distorts the fellowship between us and our heavenly parent, our Heavenly Father.

As I sit here staring at the misty rainbow that forms from the spray of water flowing across the rock, it becomes more vivid to me. Each color of the bow is a sure promise from the Lord that I get the connection through the baptism of His Spirit. For an old hillbilly from Almost Heaven, Brother Simms has the wisdom of the ages.

Masked in Ballengee

As I sway back and forth in the old rocker here on the porch of the little cabin in the meadow, I find tiny beads of sweat starting their journey down my neck. Usually, a breeze is coming up from the valley of the Greenbrier, but the air has been still for the past two days. Yesterday, I was musing that the sparrows ran further across the lawn to gain flight into the atmosphere. Yesterday, Saturday, was a record-breaking day for the temperature here in the Almost Heaven Ballengee. Eighty-seven degrees are forcing me to move the old rocker to a shaded portion of the porch. Saturday is when the little woman churns the milk to make the butter spread over the cornbread, but the heat is so high that she declares that we could use some of the preserves from the cellar. As I stirred the air, rocking back and forth in the rocker, I watched the sun peek over the East Ridge in its golden glory.

I know that the Lord was putting on another display of His magnificent glory to herald on this day, the first day of the week, the day to travel to His house to praise Him for the blessings that He bestows. I was thinking that instead of putting on my heavy bib overalls and leather boots. I would search the closet for slacks, loafers, and a dress shirt. I knew that the air would be still inside the Church, and the heat would become unbearable with fifteen or twenty, ninety-eight-degree bodies heating the air further. We have stained glass at the Church, and I knew that Homer Massey and Johnny Crawford would be in a debate.

With the windows closed, the stained glass would block the sun's rays and not be so hot upon the folks in the pews. But if the windows were open, what slight breeze from the Greenbrier would be very welcome. I can see it all now as Homer is always the first to arrive, opening the windows and Johnny coming in behind him and closing the windows. I nearly wish to see the argument between the two, knowing that Brother Simms would have to settle it with a decision. Poor Brother Simms, I thought as the little woman called out from the kitchen, "Breakfast!"

I hadn't expected that as I had not smelled the aroma of bacon frying on the stove, heard the scraping metal while the eggs were being turned, the stirring of the grits, and no sound of the toaster popping out the toast. This lack of sensation only excited me to move into the dining area and explore the marvels of a piping hot country breakfast. As the children and I sat at the table, my better half came in with a pot of oatmeal and strawberries. It was good; the strawberries were sweet but not the breakfast I had dreamed of for a Sunday morning.

The morning shadows were still tall as we descended the meadow path. I would slow in the areas where the sun was beating down to not work up to that uncomfortable residue of sweat on the skin. Then, I would slow when the tall oaks were wide and, providing shade, covered the path. My slothful conservative pace would cause the woman to shout back at me, adding that we would be late for Sunday school. See the Cardinals, she said. They are going about their morning duties and getting their work done. I could not argue the point, so I did the wise thing and just said hum. "My, how the honeysuckle has flavored the meadow with its sweet aroma this morning."

I somehow found myself in that imaginary debate between Homer and Johnny while rocking on the porch. When we reached the hard road, there was no shade as the direction had changed, and the sun was climbing higher, shortening the distance of the shade. With the new morning's sun taking a greater aim at our little convoy, the little woman said I hope Homer hasn't opened the windows and let all this warm air into the Church. In my foolishness, I somehow took a different direction and said I hope Johnny has opened the windows. The reply was that all the pews have fans, and we do not need to let the sunlight in and bake us during the service. Those thoughts never concluded, and I knew this debate would not have a satisfying answer either. So I changed the subject and said, let us take our time and admire this beautiful creation about us that God has given us to enjoy. That worked until we got to the Church and saw the windows shut. I felt as if Brother Simms had let me down.

Brother Simms and the menfolk gathered in the rear of the Church for our class, but the double doors of the Church were left open. Brother Simms mentioned that the Church's back windows were also open in hopes that a breeze would come up from the Greenbrier. As Brother Simms was discussing his meditation on Matthew 5:3, ***Blessed are the poor in spirit, for theirs is the kingdom of heaven,*** I found myself listening to the sound of churning water rushing over the rocks in the Greenbrier. It was a pleasant backdrop to the discussion and reminded me of the power that God holds in His hand.

After Sunday school, we all went out in hopes of some cooler air and wondering where Brother John could be. It is not like Brother John to be late; he gives us the word most Sundays. As time drew near for the service, even Brother Simms became fidgety. Then, just in time, Brother John came up the path from the hard road, and our fears were relieved. If there were a saint's saint, it would be have to be Brother John. Advanced in maturity is how we at the Church on the Knoll say it for a man who is an elder to us all. I don't know any of the stories, but if one in our flock has a life question or is going through a complex trial, it is Brother John they would seek out for his wise thoughts.

There was a difference in Brother John's appearance this Sunday. Brother John usually wore a skimmer hat, a white shirt with a black bow tie, black knit trousers, and polished leather tie-up shoes. It was his standard appearance for each Sunday that he attended. Brother John wore a suit and tie on one of the hottest Sundays. It was a pinstriped, dark-colored suit and a white shining silk tie. Never has any of us seen Brother John dressed that way. The little woman asked me if there was a funeral this Sunday. I didn't think so, but I replied that Brother John sure looked grand.

If there is an angel of the Church at the Church on the Knoll, it most certainly is Brother John. As I have always said, he is not a dynamic speaker, but his insight into God's word is always new and fresh, teaching us more about how we should live in the image of our Lord and Savior, Jesus Christ. This week, Brother John spoke on Psalm 51:17, which reads. ***The sacrifices of God are a broken spirit; A broken and a contrite heart, O God, You will not despise.*** (Psalm 51:17). It seemed that it would fit right in with our Sunday school lesson given to us by Brother Simms. But as I said, Brother John went in a different direction than I expected.

After his message, he took a turn that I would never have expected a teacher of God's Word to take. People, I think, when they view a teacher, see him as the example they are to follow. We all know the foolishness of that, as there is only one example: the life of Jesus. But it is human nature to follow the best example we have. The Israelite people followed Moses. When I was in first grade, the teacher could do no wrong, and I believed everything she taught me. We all have had role models as we pass along the way. It is human nature to affix ourselves to people we hold high esteem for. As I said here at the Church on the Knoll, Brother John is a saint's saint. But we were surprised to hear of all the struggles that Brother John was going through. And some of the darker things that he had done in his life. He finished by saying that he was a broken man.

Brother John removed his shoes and revealed tattered socks that his toes were showing through. He pulled out that shiny silk tie, and the bottom of it was cut off. Brother John removed his pinstriped suit coat, and his shirt was shredded. He took off his glasses and ran his fingers through where the lenses were supposed to be. Brother John looked at us all in his fatherly way and said, "I've made my point. From there, Brother John walked out of the Church, and the service was over.

Again, I find myself moving to and fro in the old rocker here on the porch of my cabin in the meadow. I am still trying to pull the day together and at a loss. We all wear our masks, but God knows. We smile at people while hiding our tears. When asked how our day has been, we answer, "Never been better." When trouble comes into our lives, we retreat behind closed doors so that no one else will know we are having trouble. But God knows, and He cares. Perhaps if we took off the mask we wear, the people who love and care for us would allow the love of God to shine through, and they would give us what we need: their own experience with the same problems. But I fear that in our quiet times with our Lord, who knows, do we remove the mask? As I ponder these thoughts, I realize God knows better than we do what we are going through because He has been through it and overcame it. My Bible was open as I prepared to go into the cabin, and I read this verse. ***Come to Me, all who are weary and heavy-laden, and I will give you rest. Take My yoke upon you and learn from Me, for I am gentle and humble in heart, and you will find rest for your souls.*** (Matthew 11:28-29)

<u>Scotty's Offering</u>

It was another glorious morning about to give birth to another wonderful Sunday here in the Almost Heaven of Ballengee. I found myself in my usual spot each early morning, rocking back and forth in the old rocker. As the eastern sky began to show its promise of a coming sunrise, I found myself musing over the events of the prior evening. Now and then, my thoughts would pause the interruption of the iron skillet ringing out the sound of its placement upon the old wood stove, growing the anticipation of the flavor of frying bacon filling the early air of the day. Last evening, Johnny Crawford visited with his oldest boy, Scotty. Scotty had just returned from his adventures in Charlotte the day before, attending school there. Like so many young folks here in Ballengee, he had left the country life to seek fame and fortune in the greater cities of opportunity. As he often said, Scotty was studying architecture and dreamed of building significant structures to admire more civilized people than the simple country folk.

Johnny was so proud to show him off, and I must say that Scotty was growing into a fine-looking young man of the world from which he had been visiting. His whole demeanor was far from the simple ways of those who work their farms and spend the weekends amongst friends and family. Often, we would find ourselves relaxing along the banks of the Greenbrier with a pole in hand, trying to catch an evening meal. Oh, the excitement of gathering on a large porch, listening to the rhythms of a local bluegrass band singing of the country life and exploding into those great old gospel hymns. Then, there are the quieter times of listening to the ladies chat and sit in a circle sewing a quilt or snapping pole beans while the men challenge themselves to a game of checkers. That would not be complex enough for a boy like Scotty Crawford to satisfy his desire to reach higher goals. Johnny is proud of his son for reaching out for far loftier stations in life, and when I ponder the fact, I am also proud of Scotty.

As I look off into the east, the sun begins to display the brilliance of God's glory across the heavens. Just beyond the Greenbrier, the sun has made its bright golden spender from behind the eastern mountains of the far country. The majesty of the bright gold creating images of reddish-orange beneath the floating clouds is a picture of beauty that only a loving heavenly Father could grant to these old eyes of mine.

After breakfast, the best half and I made our journey down the path in the meadow from our cabin to our usual residence on Sunday at the Church on the Knoll. As I have said before, there are five Churches in Ballengee, and four of them have members of a hundred or more each Sunday. I prefer the smaller bunch at the Church on the Knoll as we are more than any other place I have worshipped an intimate Church family. I know other Churches are as well, but people come and go thinking the grass is greener somewhere other than where they are. At the Church on the Knoll, everybody is there; if not, there is a great concern about why. Not that we are nosey people, but if a family member is missing, we want to know they are alright. Such a disappearance was found when I arrived at the Church.

The day prior, Brother Simms called Brother John to tell him he would be out of town this Sunday. I was hurt that I didn't know of the occurrence, but how would I, as I do not have a phone? I'm not too fond of having a party line where anyone could pick up their phone and listen in. Generally, if I am talking behind someone's back, I like it to stay there. We all have our personal opinions, and I know that most of the time, that is where they should stay, personal. Then again, I do not need the temptation to pick up the phone and hear everything that goes on in other people's lives. A phone may be necessary, but it is mostly just social media and nothing more than a tool for gossip. I like the idea that if I want to talk to someone, I should make an effort to go and speak face to face. We tend to speak more truthfully, and the effort is more rewarding.

Brother Simms always delivers the word to us each Sunday, and it would seem very inadequate without him standing behind the pulpit. We have indeed come to worship our Lord. Still, it is never the same when the regular deliverer is absent. Many Churches find that people do not come when the preacher is away, and I know that is wrong, but that is still the way it is. I have said before that there is nothing dynamic in how Brother Simms delivers the word, but no one can deliver more like a loving father to a child than Brother Simms. I knew Brother John would deliver the word, but it is still not the same. I quickly overcame my selfishness and realized it is God's garden, and I should rejoice and be glad.

After Sunday school, we moved to the front of the Church and prepared for the morning worship service. Brother John opened with a prayer, and then we sang a few hymns. Reba Maxwell was at her usual best on the piano, and Sister Mary played her mandolin, filled with great acoustic sound. Rose Maxwell led us all in the vocals. Then Brother John prayed as we prepared our hearts to receive the word from the Almighty Creator of the Heavens and the Earth.

Brother John gave us the Scripture for his message, Mark 12:4-44. I quickly glanced over the verses and saw that it was the story of the Poor Window who gave her last mite into the treasury of the Temple. It made sense to me that this would be Brother John's path this morning. Brother John is the one who takes care of the money in the Church, so who better than him to give a message on stewardship? Brother Simms would never give such a message as he knows that each of us here depends entirely on the welfare of the farms in the community. As it is, we are folks of moderate means, yet we are satisfied, and none of us are in want of our needs.

Brother John began his message by speaking of Jesus' observation that the Poor Widow had given all she had to the treasury. She gave in faith, and she held nothing back to provide the tomorrows that would follow. Then Brother John shifted the focus to the power of one mite. He told us how Jesus had prayed throughout the night before choosing His disciples. How the twelve had gone on after Jesus went home to the Father, and today, millions of Christians worldwide exist. The power of the mite is duplication, and we are to go and make disciples in all world nations. But he said that it began with prayer and that prayer is the foundation for all God can do through us. Brother John closed with this thought that the gift we have the most of is our time. How much of our time do we give back to the Lord? He finished with this: we should pray for those who do not care for the word of God, that their hearts would be opened to the gospel message, and that they, too, would find their way home through Jesus. As dissatisfied as I had approached the service without Brother Simms, Brother John gave a stunning message.

Then Homer Massy and Fred Meaders came forward with the offering plates to collect the morning's offering. I went to the Church with four quarters in my pocket and gave one of them at Sunday school. I planned to provide two more for the worship service. As I pulled the three out of my pocket, I looked at them and remembered that we planned to stop on the way home and get each an ice cream cone. I decided that I would go ahead and put all three quarters into the plate. I don't know if the Lord was pleased, but it did make my conscience feel better.

Before Brother John could say the offering prayer from the back of the Church, but Scotty Crawford came forward and stood in front of Brother John. Scotty asked Brother John for one of the offering plates, and Brother John handed him one. Scotty then placed the plate on the floor, and its sound echoed throughout the Church.

We were all very curious as to what this boy was doing. Scotty then balanced himself on the rims of the plate. Once he steadied himself, he looked up at Brother John and said, "Preacher, I give myself as an offering to the Lord."

I now find myself in my place of retirement, swaying to and fro in the old rocker much as my thoughts travel to the fore and aft of my mind. I know that someday, when we all reach the yonder shore, the books will be opened, and each must give an account of the stewardship of our time, talent, and treasure. It will be a day of great anxiety for some, while it will be a day of rest for others. I know for myself I have fallen way short of the glory of God, yet where there is the breath of life within, there still is hope for me. I am amazed that the closing thoughts of my day are influenced by a young man who went off from home to conquer the world. He returned home to find his victory in Jesus, to whom he had given his all. So often, many of us go off into the far country to win the war already won. Yet, many continue to try and achieve it for themselves. Then, the fortunate sons find themselves in the right place for their visitation from the King. They surrender and gain a victory from the Master, who will surely lead them all the way home.

A Wind Led Kite

It has been a perfect day here in the Almost Heaven of Ballengee. Yes, the day has had its portion of challenges, disappointments, joy seasoned with sorrow, and a good fellowship between humanity, creation, and the Creator. As I sit here on the porch, swaying to and fro in the old rocker, I review the day's events, which happens to be May Day. May Day is an old European holiday to celebrate the coming spring. Spring is a welcome time after cool to cold days and nights through the winter season. Now, we see the newness of leaves forming in the trees. The buds of flowers push their way to the surface to gather the sun and share their nectar with the honeybees. Soon, their magnificent color will please the eyes of young ladies who want summer love. Soon, they will grow and be filled by the passing wind, and they will clap for the joy that summer is near. Still, there is a faint nip on the breeze as it whips across the valley trapped between the mountains. The birds have spent the day fluttering about in search of the early worm who has drawn nearer to the warmth of the dirt in the sun.

With its little nip of chill, that drifting wind caught my attention on this peaceful evening overlooking the meadow. The meadow sloops down to the hardstand that runs through the town of Ballengee, and it promises to be filled with wildflowers and lined at its borders with honeysuckle to sweeten the air. As the bright orange sun begins to bury its warmth behind the horizon, the sounds of gayety drift up from Ballengee. The smell of outdoor feast cooking and the laughter of children playing wildly in the coming evening. The town folk have ventured into their yards with guitars, violins, and banjos to play the rhythms that bring joy to the new season.

The wind rattled the cage of memory from not so long ago when the boys, Pierce, Spence, and I sought to fly our kites at the Church on the Knoll's yard, and many years ago, the men of the Church worked hard to flatten the ground to form a flat place for a cemetery at the Church. After over a hundred years, the cemetery is yet to be filled. There is plenty of room left for Church picnics, baseball games, and other outside events. Once a month, on the fourth Sunday, the Church Family will gather for a potluck supper, a time for good fellowship, trying out new recipes, and Church Family Fellowship Dinners. In the summer months, we sometimes have family camping for the whole family. Everyone pitches a tent, cooks on an open fire, works on woodland crafts, and tell stories in the evenings by a campfire.

It's a great place to fly a kite. In the early years, Pierce, Spence, and I would go and fly kites. One year, we have a contest to see who can get their kite to fly the highest. I would always win, and the little woman would get upset. "How could they be better if I always let them win," I would tell her. In the later years, that was not the case, and I was proud to lose. The competition began the first year we went flying the kites. Even though the kids could not get their kites higher than mine at first, their attitude was the usual; "wow." "Gee, dad, you are good." I would dream they would go to the other kids at school saying; my dad can beat your dad flying kites. I often expected Ken Martin to come by one day and challenge me.

The kite-flying contest lasted one year. Spence was very determined to at least best Pierce. I watched Spence practicing running very fast without really looking where he was going. I told him to watch out for doing that. I said you would not run backward without looking, would you? But he was determined and willing to take the risk.

The three of us stood at the backside of the graveyard with our kites swinging in the breeze. I'd wait for a puff of wind and let more string out. Pierce would notice the technique and try the same. Developing the anticipation was hard, but he was getting the hang of it. Spence was not that patient and took off running to create some resistance. As expected, he was not watching the direction he was going and ran underneath a tree branch. The kite became quickly entangled in a branch of the tree.

We all tried to wiggle the kite free, but it was about fifteen feet in the air, hanging over a limb. Every time we pulled the string, the limb would catch the kite's tail. Pierce somehow gets the idea that he will be Spence's hero, climb up the tree, and free the kite. I didn't quite like that idea, considering the kite only cost fifty cents and a trip to the clinic was never less than fifty dollars. So instead of doing the practical thing, going to Lou's five and dime and getting a new kite, I said I would climb up and get the trapped kite.

After I reached the second branch of my mansion, I began to think that maybe I shouldn't have tried to be a hero myself. It is funny how easy things have become impossible over the years. Pride always gets in the way of common sense. So I kept on keeping on and reached a branch about a hundred feet up. Well, that's the way it felt, but it was only ten feet. Not enough to kill me, but certainly enough to hurt. The problem was solved as there was no other branch I could reach to hang on to. Pierce yelled and said, climb it like shimming up a rope. I rejected that notion and said I'm coming down, and we will go to Lou's and get a new kite. It seemed the smart thing to do, but it presented another problem. It was climbing down. Going down was more complicated than going up because of the view. There is no end to the height looking up, but when looking down, all I could see was the sudden stop should I slip.

When climbing up, you can see what you want to latch on to, and when you are going down the tree trunk, your feet and whole body block your vision. When you're climbing down, you notice the wind is swaying the trunk of the tree, and it causes you to pause with each move. Climbing down ten feet looks much further than when you look up. When climbing down, it is hard to look graceful while in complete fright.

Some do not think that the good Lord has a sense of humor. But that day at the Church on the Knoll, the Lord revealed that He enjoys a good laugh. After I managed to get one foot on solid ground and my swagger returned to my presence, a strong puff of wind came from who knows where and lifted the kite and shot it high into the sky above us. Spence was thrilled and joyfully shouted as he cheered, "My kite is higher than yours ever was. The little bragger was still holding the string as he pulled it, and the kite was so high that we could not read Superman's yellow S on its face. It was not hard for me to be scratched and weary, thankful to be on the ground and proud of my youngest son.

Sitting here in the quiet breeze of the rocker moving back and forth, I can't help but find a conclusion to that day so long ago. It's really simple yet profound. We go through life and often attempt to do what we know is not prudent. We charge ahead, thinking we have complete control and it will work out as planned. I've done that many times, and I have been shamed, failed, and humbled. As the creak of the old rocker signals the crickets chirp, I remember what I was once told is a good life verse. Proverbs 3:5-6. ***Trust in the LORD with all your heart And do not lean on your own understanding. In all your ways acknowledge Him, And He will make your paths straight.*** For much of my life, I have had the "I got this" attitude." I often find out that it is far from the truth. In our dominion of God's creation in this world, we must give Him the glory in all we do with His creation. If nothing else, it is courtesy.

When we dance outside His will, we had best include Him, or what we do may not end well. From the minute to the magnificent, if you think about that, then from the minute to the magnificent requires the grace and mercy of God's blessing. We often wonder why it didn't work out, and should we? If God is not in it, then why would He bless it? God does have a sense of humor, and I am sure He is amused, but I am not sure I want Him laughing at me. We cannot control His creation try as we must, but do not wonder when it fails. His Spirit is our counselor, and He knows the path we should be on. ***The wind blows where it wishes and you hear the sound of it, but do not know where it comes from and where it is going; so is everyone who is born of the Spirit.*** (John 3:8)

<u>Agnes</u>

I find myself again in the old rocker, creaking to the mysteries that will unfold before I retire to the inner sanctuary of my room. There to find solace from the day in the confidence of the little woman who guides me away from insanity with whispers of love and statements of God's Truth. As I look to the west over the small valley before the mountain, I see the little lights blinking from the living rooms of neighbors' homes and wonder what treasures are slipping through their hearts. Here on the porch nestled in the rocker, the treasure of the day reveals itself as a blessing to harbor evermore.

I look above the small valley and note the darkening midnight blue in the sky and the explosive, bright orange-red color forming the outline of the west mountain. How beautiful the blending of deep blue and the brightness of orange and red glow set the atmosphere of my thoughts on this somber day. It could have been the day that drives my thoughts, but I believe they began long ago when I was a five-year-old exploring the limits of the boundaries of Ballengee. These boundaries have held me tucked close to this day spent at the funeral home.

When I was five and almost well-behaved, or when my older brothers or sister would not attend, my mother would take me on adventures as she moved about in Ballengee. This day was the first time I remember going to Aunt Agnes' house. I was excited as I thought this would be something new and very different. Aunt Agnes was my father's sister, and my mind vaguely remembers her before this day's adventure. We went there so my mom could have her hair fixed. My mom was a straight-haired lady, but when we went to Aunt Agnes, she would come out of the hairdryer with curls. At first, my jaw would drop in unbelief, and everyone there would laugh. Perhaps it was a funny look to them, or the bright blush seemed comical. I picked up a magazine to hide behind, only to be looking at women's clothes. The folks there only laughed louder. Aunt Agnes scolded them, and they quieted down.

As the years passed and I grew to an older age of seven or eight, I could cross streets, and the borders of my world became larger and larger. Often, I would go to Aunt Agnes', as she always had hot chocolate ready for me to enjoy. We always had interesting conversations, and I loved how she understood what I was discussing. I had never met an older person who could know so much about kid things and relate to their kid days. As the years have continued to travel on, Aunt Agnes and I have had millions of conversations, and I have always come away a bit wiser.

After my first day in junior high, I was terrified. My wonderful world of elementary school was over. There is a lot of difference between being suitable for one teacher and now having six. There is a lot of difference between one set of friends and now having six.

After that first day, I went to talk to Aunt Agnes. She would remember back then, and she would know what to do. I told Aunt Agnes. It wasn't suitable to place me in such a confusing place with so many people to learn. Why can't the school find a teacher smart enough to teach all the stuff I needed, like in elementary? I told Aunt Agnes how afraid, confused, and worried I was. Aunt Agnes just listened to my rant, and I thought she would be just like Mom and say I had to go. But she didn't. She let me tell everything I had to say and never stopped me.

Aunt Agnes then looked at me and smiled, assuring me. She reminded me how my mom brought me here that first time. Then she asked how I got there that day. I answered that I know the way, I know the streets, and I know her house. She asked me how I knew all of that. I said because I grew up and can find my way. Aunt Agnes then asked the big question. Do you always want to be in grade school, or do you want to find your way?

In my ninetieth year, I was scared that my whole life would be working on my father's farm. The older man at Hillsdale Dairy said he would teach me to drive the delivery truck and travel all over Summers County delivering milk. I told my dad what I wanted to do, and he had a fit. Dad said he could not afford to lose me working for him. It made me feel guilty, so I passed the opportunity. Later, it began to bother me that I would never do anything else but grow food and shovel chicken specs.

I went over to Aunt Agnes and told her my fear of letting my dad down. Aunt Agnes asked why I feared my dad. I don't want to let him down, and I don't want to him to lose his farm. Aunt Agnes asked if I thought my father wanted me to be happy and if he wanted me to be my own man. I thought about that for a while and said yes, he does. Aunt Agnes then said, do what I believe is right. I worked on that advice for a few days. I told my dad I was unhappy being a farmer and wanted to try new things to build my life. He was initially sad, but then he changed and said he was proud of me. He said I want you to be you, now go. I got that job, and it grew to driving a truck nationwide.

My stories of Aunt Agnes could go on throughout the night and maybe the year. I never once in all those years had the chance to tell her how significant her influence was on my life. Now, after today, I never will, as today I was at her funeral.

The Church on the Knoll was packed today. I have never seen so many people try to squeeze into that old one-room Church. My eldest brother gave the eulogy, and Brother Massey said the devotion. As I sat there with my family, the children, and siblings, I was saddened that my children would never have the blessing of Aunt Agnes' wisdom. Through the service, I could hear the small whimpers, the near-silent sniffles, and the glance of people reaching for a tissue. Somehow, I could not find grief within; I could not flow a tear out, and I did not feel deep sorrow. All I could muster was a sense of well-being in my soul.

The casket was open, which I hate. My last look at someone does not need to be when that person is not there to look back. My final impression is not when they are lifeless but when they are full of life. Someone had placed a dark curtain over the stained glass windows, making it darker than ever before in the little Church. The only thing of beauty was the flowers that had been placed. Brother Massey, in his devotional, quoted a verse from Isaiah, ***The grass withers, the flower fades, But the word of our God stands forever.*** (Isaiah 40:8). I thought he made the correct point when he said Agnes was a beautiful woman because the Word of God ruled her heart. All I could think was so true, so true.

As the light fades into the darkness behind the west mountain and the stars blossom across the evening sky, I ask myself what victory is. I remember the words of my mother that she pounded into me time and time again. Your victory is in Jesus and only Jesus. Somehow, that visits me now and then, and tonight is one of them. Years ago, I came home from Southeast Asia. I was disillusioned that I hadn't gone there to win a war, just to fight one. Now, the only one who seemed to understand me had traveled on and left me behind. The siblings have moved away, and the kids are finding their way. I root for them, but I am not in their way.

After I came home from Southeast Asia, I went to see Aunt Agnes. I first noticed she had aged as much as I had over that year. I felt terrible when she asked about my time there. I spoke of it with none other, and I still care not to today from so long ago. I told her I faced off against my share of those on the other side, but they were not my greatest enemy. Aunt Agnes said she knows, as she fights the same battle each day. That was the marvelous truth about Aunt Agnes; she knows me. I asked her how you won against yourself. She answered, what did your mother say? Victory is only in Jesus, I answered. How do you win, Aunt Agnes? She didn't hesitate with her answer as she knew it by heart. Aunt Agnes' answer is how I found peace at her funeral today. The same answer gives me peace every day when I battle myself. Every time I sit on this porch swaying back and forth in the rocker, I have the victory due to what she said. My mom was right; victory is only in Jesus, and Aunt Agnes provides a vital key. ***Finally, brethren, whatever is true, whatever is honorable, whatever is right, whatever is pure, whatever is lovely, whatever is of good repute, if there is any excellence and if anything worthy of praise, dwell on these things.*** (Philippians 4:8)

As I sit here pondering in the old rocker, wondering about the treasures the neighbors of the valley have discovered this evening, I know the treasure I have received. For Agnes, all those glorious thoughts she had pondered throughout her years had come home to her. ***I, the LORD, search the heart, I test the mind, Even to give to each man according to his ways, According to the results*** (Jeremiah 17:10)

Mary Macbeth

It is a pleasant day here in the Almost Heaven of Ballengee. I find myself sitting on a rock along the riverside of the Greenbrier River, listening to the rhythm of water making its way south to the Kanawha. The Greenbrier is not a deep river that flows over a bed of rocks but has deeper places along its course. There is a place not far from where I now ponder that we jumped from a ledge into the river in our younger days. The challenge was how many flips one could make, landing headfirst into the river. Somehow, I couldn't flip and would land on my belly or feet first. The former is remembered, and the latter is most desired.

Today, as I look down at the smaller rocks with the water swirling around, I notice a familiar creature called Crawdaddys from my youth. I don't know what they are actually. Back then, that is what everyone called them. They are miniature Lobster-looking creatures with pinchers on long arms to capture their prey or defend themselves from boys like me. I never intended to harm the Crawdaddys, and their pinch was not all that painful unless they pinched between the fingers.

The one Crawdaddy I was watching came out from the crevasse of a rock, and when my shadow came across him, he would dash back beneath the rock. I would move back, and he would come out, and when I moved forward, he would hide. I soon lost interest in this game but wondered what secrets were hidden in his safe place. I can't explain why, but the memory of Mary Macbeth comes to mind. It was as if the Crawdaddy brought out that memory from my safe place.

Mary Macbeth, my Mary Macbeth, her memory at one time was painful for my heart to recall. Today, with so many years passed by, Mary's memory brings warmth to my heart. She was my first love one where I fell hook, line, and sinker. My young heart as a senior in High School was filled with the allure of Mary Macbeth. The first time my eyes were filled with the lust of Mary was on the second-floor balcony of the school. I stood there looking below, waiting for the time I would have to enter the classroom. Then, suddenly, she was walking through the courtyard to some unknown class at school. I watched every step, hoping she would look up and see me. Then, I was afraid she would see me observing her every move.

Since then, I have never believed in love at first sight. Love takes time, as there is more to learn than appearances. But at seventeen, I was all about appearances, and Mary Macbeth had them all. I had never seen anyone walk the way that Mary did. I can't explain it, but her special stroll pulled my heart into her cadence. Every day, I would rush to the balcony to watch Mary Macbeth stroll by below. Her far view filled my heart until, finally, it was nearly busting over.

I asked all my friends if they knew who she was or anything about her. I wandered the campus searching for Mary but never found her. I even went to see the dean about her. A place I would never voluntarily go. I tried as casually as possible to ask the dean, do you know what class Mary Macbeth is in right now? The dean would not answer that question. I had to meet her somehow.

I am not a social person, as I had my farm chores after school. I found unexpected energy and rushed through the chores each night to go to the local hangout. Finally, on Saturday night, she was sitting with a bunch of guys from Talcott of all places. I went over and sat as close as possible, hoping someone I knew would come in to start a loud conversation. As fate would have it, no one I knew came in that night. I was trying to think of something distractive that would catch her eye. I once saw a guy who took three straws and balanced them to stand up. Then he placed his drink on the straws, which stayed there. I thought that was amazing, and I tried doing that.

I got three paper straws that had been unused so they would not be soft. After many futile attempts, they stood straight up on the table. Then I took the paper cup filled with cherry cola and carefully placed it on the straws. I did it but kept my hands near the cup to be sure. The cup remained secure in place. I moved my hands away as I looked to see if Mary Macbeth was watching. I should not have allowed the distraction of looking at her as my elbow shook when I turned my head. The cup fell and poured cherry cola all down the front of my pants. Mary Macbeth watched me as I stood up, looking like the fool I was.

Mary Macbeth was in the cafeteria on Monday at school when I went in before school. She had never been there before when I came to school. I wanted so badly to go over, but I was too embarrassed. Mary came over to my table, and in disbelief, I must have blushed brightly. Mary said I should have stayed Saturday night as the whole place laughed long after I left over what I had done. Not what I wanted to hear, but she was talking to me. We talked a little while over simple stuff, and I was trying to keep that going. It was getting to be time for class, so I did something even more stupid to be with her. I suggested we go down to the Greenbrier and have a day off. I couldn't believe it. She said yes. It was the best day I had ever had, and we had a wonderful time getting to know each other. So I thought. When I asked her to the sock hop Friday night, she said she was going, but with her steady. I was crushed.

My sorrow did not end there. On Monday after school, my best friend Johnny Crawford saw my dad on the way home from school. Johnny asked my dad if I was feeling all right. In that conversation, my dad realized I was not at school Monday. When I got home, it was a trip to the woodshed. I had never in my life been so consumed with a girl, never been so in love that there was nothing else I could think about. Never a girl that I was willing to make a fool of myself several times to get her attention. All the many nights of anticipation were blown in an instant. It was not that she had a steady. Mary Macbeth's steady was Johnny Crawford, my best friend.

As I was pondering through this now fond memory, which taught me the difference between lust and love, Brother Simms came drifting by on a raft. He paddled over to the shore for a visit on a pleasant afternoon along the Greenbrier. Brother Simms asked what I was doing, so I told him the short version. I was thinking about my first love and what a fool I made of myself over it. Brother Simms, in his usual way, said something simple but profound. "Yeah, some are fools for first love, some for possession, and some for Jesus. It's not bad to be foolish when it is the right cause." I had to agree. It's more manageable now that Mary Macbeth was fifty-two years past me. It was then painful, but now it is a beautiful memory of learning a good lesson.

It's now Sunday evening, and you know where I am. Swaying towards and against the evening breeze drifting up the meadow. I examine Brother Simms's message today at the Church in the Knoll. And compare it to the lesson learned from a memory of years ago by the Greenbrier Saturday afternoon just past. Brother Simms spoke out of the book of Revelation, chapter two, verses four, and five. ***"But I have this against you, that you have left your first love. 'Therefore remember from where you have fallen, and repent and do the deeds you did at*** first; ***or else I am coming to you and will remove your lampstand out of its place--unless you repent."*** (Revelation 2:4-5)

I cannot remember all Brother Simms said today, but as I think about the verses, I don't believe the Lord said I had left my first love. I truly loved Mary Macbeth with all my heart. If I had never met her face to face, it would have been enough to stand on that balcony and watch her pass each day. I know I have my wife and kids, my job, and I love pondering on the porch of the little cabin, but none are my first love. Then there is the Crawdaddy of my youthful memories that I loved down by the Greenbrier, but the Crawdaddy is not my first love. However, he lived by the small rock and would see by my shadow. He would retreat into the rock and bring out the more profound things to reveal to me in my mind.

The first love of all humanity should be the truest of love, that love that brings all into existence and provides all that humanity needs to live. The most important of which is His love. As I move to and fro in the old rocker, swaying back and forth in the wind of the Spirit, my first love is the One who loved me even before I was. Therefore, I try these days to keep His commandment as best I can, hoping that someday I will be with my first love. ***"But I have this against you, that you have left your first love. 'Therefore remember from where you have fallen, and repent and do the deeds you did at first; or else I am coming to you and will remove your lampstand out of its place--unless you repent."*** (Revelation 2:4-5)

Peace Completed

It's that beautiful time of the year when I have moved the old rocker inside next to the fireplace in the living room of the little cabin. The kids are busy in their rooms preparing for the lessons of school they will learn tomorrow. I was surprised at how quickly they had grown from the first day I turned them over to the world. That first day of school, that first grade, and the first time they were not in the middle of our daily life. Miss Mary wanted to stay with them that first day to assure herself that the teacher would treat them with the love and concern she had over their first five years. Necessary as it was, it was a painful letting go to see them pass through the large doors into a world filled with possibilities unknown. Now Pierce is a senior, Spence is a junior, and Victoria is a sophomore in high school. Soon, life will carry them away, and the family name will be carried away from them. I am crossed with pride and impending loneliness, a slash in two directions.

I listen to the snapping sparks fly into the chimney to warm the coldness of the wind, which also slithers through the non-caulked windows. Another honey-do job left undone. Sometimes, one must reap what is not sown. The snow was coming down when I went to work today, and I did not take my goulashes. Tomorrow, I must try to master them, as I know the paths in the snow will turn to slush if the sun gives warmth to the cold air. They were my father's goulashes; he'd wear them with his pants tucked neatly inside. I have never mastered that because I could never get the metal buckles together. Oh, if I had only observed him on the past snowy days. Now, I wear them with the buckles undone, and the breeze flows into the openings of the goulashes and freezes my feet. We live and learn but fail to be obedient to the lesson.

I left work early that day to attend the funeral of a friend's son, Joe Rippetoe. I knew his father, Carl, many years ago when I was seven and in the mid-'50s. At that time, he was bedridden and unable to care for himself. Mrs. Rippetoe did her best, and I met her one day while walking around the neighborhood. She was a squatty person who carried a broad smile across her face. She always had a kind word to share, and I enjoyed greeting her as I made my rounds. One day, I asked her where Mr. Rippetoe was and then felt sad when she answered. She told me that he was bedridden and was not able to get up. Later, she let me know that he would never get better. I could not understand that, except I thought he would live his life out stuck in the bed.

As time passed, it bothered me that Mr. Rippetoe was alone in that bed all day. One day, I asked Mrs. Rippetoe if I could come in and visit him. She said to come back tomorrow and would think about that and let me know. I did, and she said yes and let me into the house. I didn't know what I was getting into, and once inside, I felt afraid and shy. I started thinking of excuses that would let me out without hurting any feelings. I have always been a slow thinker; no excuse came in time. Mrs. Rippetoe said to go upstairs with her, and I did.

When I was allowed into Mr. Rippetoe's room, I found myself in an amazing place. I introduced myself, and he said his name was Carl. He was in a huge bed that had buttons along the bedrails. He could push the buttons, and the front of the bed would rise up or down. Another button that the whole bed would raise up or down. There was a button to make the bed vibrate, and I liked sitting on it when it vibrated. All around the walls, there were bookcases filled with books. I looked at some of them, and they had pictures. Most of the photographs were of pigs. I figured Carl liked pigs the same way I liked dogs.

It made sense when Carl told me he was a pig farmer near Logan's farm in Creamery. Without thinking, I said, "When you get better, we can see them." Carl smiled and said he promised to take me there as soon as possible. Carl also had some of the same books my dad had. They were Bible books, storybooks, and magazines from Grace Baptist Church in town. I asked Carl if he went to Grace Church, and he said he did. I asked if he knew Johnny Crawford, but he didn't at first. After I told Carl about my friend Johnny, he said he thought he knew of him. From then on, I would go there every day and visit Carl.

I liked being with Carl in his room, which he called his world; it was filled with many exciting books to look at. He loved to hear me tell of my adventures, and the stories he told me about the old days in Ballengee were astounding. The books were neat, and the stories were interesting. Carl was very caring even though he was decades older than me. What I liked most about visiting Carl was that his room was a place of peace. Because Carl was ill, he was a very quiet man, and I would have to listen very intently to hear all he was saying. Every time Carl would share an adventure, it would end with practical advice for my life. Carl's place was always at peace. Carl never spoke harshly or glared, and his answers always satisfied. It was even more than that, as peace reminded me of being in a Church during service. There was no fear, anxiety, or rudeness to how others treated each other. In Carl's room, I wasn't a bothersome little kid in the way of what others wanted to do. I didn't have to measure up to anyone except myself. It was peaceful because Carl knew who I was, even though I hadn't yet. Carl accepted me just as I was.

Carl always had a story that would end with advice on how to handle the problems of growing up. Then, one day, Pastor David Lamb's car was parked in front of Carl's Place. Several people were standing outside, talking in low tones. I knew, but I wanted to be told, but I just stood there, unable to speak. I wanted to cry but didn't know the reason, so I held back. Then Mrs. Rippetoe came over and told me the words I feared. She said, "Carl has gone home, and you must wait for a while. A day will come again that you can go to Carl's Place." I just looked at her through misty eyes and said, "Thank you." It has been fifty-three years since that day, and I do not remember much about Carl Rippetoe's funeral but the verse Pastor Lamb quoted. ***"Peace I leave with you; My peace I give to you; not as the world gives do I give to you. Do not let your heart be troubled, nor let it be fearful.*** (John 14:27)

Today, I went to Carl's son's funeral. I've known Joe for many years, as we would bump into each other now and then. He's a few years older than me, but we do not have much in common. I have little chance of knowing you if you are not a farmer, are not involved in the feed and seed industry, or attend the Church on the Knoll. As far as I know, he was a good man in the community, and I never heard any different. When I heard he was ill, I went to see Joe and noticed his home was not like his father's. The house was filled with confusion, noise, and arguments. The arguments were over the inheritance, and they could not agree on anything. It is sad when the blessings of life become the curse. How can one praise the Lord over His blessings and argue over receiving them? There were no bookshelves filled with exciting books and no Bible or Bible stories to be read. It was the home of a businessman chasing after the American Dream. A dream, if accomplished, is left behind at the exit.

Pastor Lamb gave the service, as at most funerals I attend, it passed into history like the one who has departed. But this one was special because the verse Pastor Lamb used in the service struck profoundly. I didn't know much about Joe, but I learned much about his father, Carl, from the verse the Pastor quoted. ***Draw near to God and He will draw near to you. Cleanse your hands, you sinners; and purify your hearts, you double-minded.*** (James 4:8)

As I sit here, warming my body with the crackling fire and ponder the day's events, I feel a warmth building in my heart. I remember those early childhood years filled with the real and imagined competition of growing up as a child trying desperately to become a man.

Being submissive to everyone taller than five feet and having your life judged by the manners you remembered to display. I was never a sportsman but was made to play. I was never a singer but was made to sing—never a leader but made to go first. I was never anything others wanted me to be. I found my peace at Carl's Place. I always thought it was Carl, always thought it was his books, and I always thought his room was the only refuge. Now, I know without a question that the peace came from the God that Carl served. God's peace filled his place because God was near to Carl because Carl was near God.

Oh, how I missed it, but now I have found it. There before me in the fondest of memory is Carl. A man was struck with a fatal illness. Counting down the days until he will leave this darkened world and, in a twinkling, find himself in the loving arms of His Lord. Carl, who suffered his last years in the prison of a bed, where most people seek rest, found it there in his last days. Carl drew near to God and, in faith, found his peace completed. ***The LORD will give strength to His people; The LORD will bless His people with peace.*** (Psalm 29:11)

A Little One's Dream

Here in Almost Heaven, spring has drifted into summer in the very short time of this week. I can already sense the rising temperature in the evening air, as it seems heavier than it was just a short time ago. Providing seed to the farms has slowed down, and my work has settled into a slower rhythm. It is a nice pause, as the hefting bags of seed soon will turn into lifting blocks of salt for the livestock to lick. Labor is the way of life at Lively's Feed Store, and I am thankful for it.

Usually, I find myself moving to and fro at dusk, rocking in the old rocker. A companion of mine since I moved into the little cabin of Tom Lively. The old rocker was resting alone on the porch, needing a friend. I obliged, and we have been pondering together ever since. Long before the discovery of the old rocker, I spent my pondering in the hammock. The old rocker brought a change in place for my hobby of pondering. Pondering is when I pause in my day, find the meaning, and store it in the corridors of my mind. Because of the gentle breeze of the evening, I have moved to the hammock.

I lay here with a gentle drift from the breeze and take note of the beauty surrounding me. The hammock has been a treasure since I can no longer count. I have often wished I had recorded the thoughts woven out from the canvas of the old hammock. There are times of blessing when they revive and excite me as a fond remembrance. Perhaps I have come to try and recapture a statement from the past to remind me of the wisdom it had shared.

The hammock is tied between two Dogwood trees in the back of the little cabin, just about twenty-five yards before the mountain starts to climb to the far horizon. It is a perfect trap for the breeze, creating a backdraft that circles back and perpetuates airflow. The gentle swaying from side to side creates a uniqueness in the acoustics of the surrounding crickets. As I drift towards the mountain, I hear their chirps directly, and as I drift back towards the cabin, I listen to their chirps with an echo. Two distinct sounds, but as I am briefly in the middle, it becomes a theater listening to a symphony. The sun before me, slipping behind the horizon, displays a spectrum of color as a tapestry painted across the heavens. No artist could create a more magnificent symphony of music against the artwork across the heavens than God Himself. I anxiously await the evening stars.

I added percussion with a folded copy of the Ballengee Record in my hand. It quickly became a distraction to the natural beauty of the moment, and I realized nothing worthy I could add more than my praise. The Ballengee Record is a small-town paper that recently started to come out two days a week, and it is still available for the fantastic price of .25 cents. Generally, the headline is what the Mayor does, which is hardly enough for two weekly printings. Then there are social activities, which we notice weeks in advance. The middle page is the editorial written by Newt Harper, who owns the paper. Then the funnies are on the back page, where I usually start my reading adventure. I enjoy Snuffy Smith the best, but Betty Mae of the Tasty Freeze writes a cute comic called "Nana Splits." I seem to think it is a witty satire of the Ballengee folk. Betty never mentions names, but we all suspect who she is talking about. Some find honor to be spoken of.

The headline in the Ballengee Record brought back some memories to mind. "Mountain State Carnival" comes to Ballengee. I've heard of the

Mountain State Carnival, and it is not a small carnival, so it would be a big deal for the town of Ballengee. The carnival will be set up at Bobcat Field on the high school grounds. The carnival will be just a weekend fling and held only on Saturday and Sunday. It would be disappointing as not many in Ballengee would spend their Sunday that way. Then Spence came out of the cabin and asked if we could spend both days at the carnival. I gave him the correct fatherly answer, "I'll think about it, son."

My answer should have been a no-brainer, but I know the times have changed since his age. I imagine Pierce and Victoria will expect a yes, just like Spence. Maybe I should have said I would have to ask your mother, but they have already been there, as she probably sent Spence to me. I remember what my dad said when Ballengee had a fair. It was a one-time adventure but unsuccessful because nobody went on a Sunday. Back then, Saturday was a workday, like Monday through Friday, and they had the fair on Sunday. Only about a hundred people went, and they never had another one.

I remember the disappointment when Dad said no. He didn't say I'll ask your mother, and he didn't say he would think about it. He just said no, and I think the difference is that my dad's no was always final. I have not developed a definitive no, and there is always a debate. Most times, well, sometimes, no holds are depending on my conviction. Maybe the problem is that my no's aren't final; my convictions aren't convicting as they should be. But the disappointment I felt with my dad's no was nearly traumatic, and I remember that night I had the craziest dream.

It was not one of those dreams that you know you had one, but you don't know what it was when you woke up. It was one of those dreams that seemed real enough that it actually happened; therefore, I remember it many years later. The next day, I told my best friend Johnny Crawford about it, and he said, "Weird." I spoke to Homer Massey about it years ago, as he is my counselor in life. Homer asked, "What does it mean to you?" I answered I didn't know, and Homer said, "Well. That is strange". I went to Brother Simms, and he gave the right idea of its purpose, but I am not sure I can employ it properly.

While still fuming after my dad's no, I went to my room and had the usual pity party. I enjoyed feeling so sorry for myself that it took a long time to fall asleep. Sleep is a sneaky thing, and you never know when you are there; you know you were when you wake up. After I fell asleep, I was somewhere I had never been before and have not since. I was walking on a small, narrow path, hearing music and laughter from other kids my age. When I came to the top of a small hill, the way ended a little farther down. When it ended, neon lights shined bright and flashed on and off. The sound of laughter and music came from beyond the gate, and a clown was standing at the gate.

While walking, I passed an older man dressed in a robe with the Word of God written on it. I stopped and asked, who are you? The old man answered, " I am the watcher of the gate." Oh, and what is that up there? I asked. He replied, "That gate is deceptive, and it is the one most people travel through. My gate few choose to pass through. It is the path to infinite joy, peace, and love. A place where learning never is finished, all is new, and creation never ends, as this place is infinite love." I asked if I could come here, and the old man answered, "No." Then I will go to the other gate, and the old man said, "No." Why can't I choose a gate? I asked. The old man answered, "It is not your time." Then his words faded until I woke up. "It is not your time - not your time."

When I spoke to Brother Simms, he said nothing at first but some scripture. Then he told me to go home and ponder that I would find the day I would need it. That Scripture was this. ***But Jesus said, Let the*** *children alone, and do not hinder them from coming to Me; for the kingdom of heaven belongs to such as these.* (Matthew 19:14)

Now, as I lay here swaying in the breeze between the chirping crickets and the re-chirping off the little cabin. I believe I have found the conviction to give Spence, Pierce, and Victoria the right answer. If I say yes or no, I have the right conviction to make my word final. Mountain State Carnival might be the day's opportunity for Ballengee, but the chance of a lifetime is to pass through the right gate.

Smoked Coffee

It has been an intriguing Saturday in the Almost Heaven of Ballengee. Now, as the evening has fallen to the darkness of night, I find myself exercising my favorite pastime, pondering while moving forward and then back in the old rocker. The wide window from the porch gives me an amazing view of the bright, star-filled night. I quickly lose myself gazing at the stars. Some stars are bright and proud in the deep, darkened sky, while others are much dimmer. As I look across the sky, the brighter stars grab all my attention. I like to put them together and create my own constellations and pictures. It's just like star gazing. As the space of time grows, I notice the pictures do not come together without using the dimmer stars. It only makes sense to me that even the smaller lights play an equal part in God's purpose. The trouble for me is when I focus on the starry sky in time, my mind drifts, and I lose my place.

My mind drifts and clings to the anchor of how the day started at Crawford's Kountry Kitchen on James Street. The celebration caused us to gather there for breakfast this morning. My youngest son Spence had arrived home from Juneau, Alaska. Brother John, Homer Massy, and Nolan came to join Johnny, Spence, and I. Johnny invited us down for some buttermilk biscuits and sausage gravy. The biscuits and gravy looked inviting, sitting next to soft Sunnyside up eggs and crispy hash brown potatoes. It was the coffee that started the conversation of the morning. Johnny always tries to say something nice, and he does, but his compliment starts a contest. Johnny said that his coffee was good but not as great as the coffee at the Church on the Knoll.

Not knowing what Johnny meant, Spence asked what was so particular about the church's coffee. Johnny replied that it was because your dad makes it, and it is Smoked Coffee. Nolan asked what in the world Smoked Coffee is, which left me to explain the art of making Smoked Coffee. I told them to get the best dark-roasted Columbian coffee beans and soak them in water overnight. Then you build a fire and let it burn down to coals. Then you take some soaked hickory wood and place it on the fire. Rinse the beans, spread them out on a large frypan, and put them on the grill. Then, you build a tent over the frypan, which traps the smoke over the beans. After the beans are dried, you grind them until they are fine. Fill the cup in the percolator and place it back on the fire. After about fifteen minutes, you will have some of the best Smoked Coffee to be had.

Each time you tell a story, there is always one in the group who has to one-up the story. I am used to that, as it must be like people making a story grander. I didn't expect that the one upper would be my son Spence. So I took the bait and asked how he found the best Smoked Coffee in Juneau, Alaska. "Oh, Dad!" he said, "In Juneau, I learned to make the best Smoked Coffee anyone could find."

Well, Dad, you have to start with the right beans. You have to get Antigua beans about two pounds. Take the beans and freeze them. Get some cherry wood, chop it into small quarters, and freeze that too. When the beans and wood are frozen, fire up the smoker with charcoal. Put the cherry wood pieces on top of the charcoal when all the charcoal is hot. Find a large cook pan and place the frozen Antigua beans in the pan. Set it in the smoker and let it smoke. The moisture in the beans will capture the flavor of the steam coming from the cherry wood and the smoke. When the beans are dried and brittle, grind it down fine. Put the coffee grinds in the percolator and let it perk, and you will have the best cherry wood-flavored Smoked Coffee. Doesn't that sound great, Dad?

Johnny and I looked across the table at each other with what we had gotten into look. We each had an expression with a thin-toothed grin. At that time, Nolan Richardson made a throated humph and pulled out his Apple Pipe and Captain Black Cherry tobacco package. He stuffed the pipe and struck a match across the tabletop. What in the heck are your young ones wasting your time over? You can't spend all day making a cup of coffee when you get my age. Go down to Lou's Five and Dime and get your desired coffee. If she doesn't have Smoked Coffee, then she will order you some.

As I rock here on the porch pondering this small adventure, it brought to my mind last Sunday's service at the Church on the Knoll. Boasting and one-upping were the topics for Brother Simm's message. The Scripture was from 2 Corinthians, which reads, ***If I have to boast, I will boast of what pertains to my weakness.*** (2 Corinthians 11:30). It was a back door entrance to saying that all that has meaning for the Kingdom of God is not our own doing but that of the Lord working through us. Brother Simms spiced the message up with some of his weaknesses, and we all realized that he was a person just like us. As Paul said somewhere in the Scripture, it is good that we should not think higher of ourselves than we ought. As Brother Simms concluded his message, Thelma Winslow stood up and came to the front of the Church.

It was kind of a Dejavu happening from this morning at the Kountry Kitchen. Thelma began to recite everything she had done in the past that she knew was not pleasing to the Lord. She kept on and on, and I became embarrassed for her and realized I had done some of the same. When Thelma had winded down, she raised her voice and mentioned her sorriness, but she was not perfect like we all are. At first, I was insulted and thought better of saying anything to anyone about the service. I found myself on the banks of the Greenbrier sorting through the service but could not balance the emotions. All I could think was poor Thelma.

Now, as I drift between the to and fro of the old rocker gazing at the stars, the brighter ones and the dimmer, I realize each plays an equal part. But I couldn't fit how Thelma thinks we are all perfect, and Thelma is the only one who is not. How some stars are brighter, and some are not. Then, some think they are perfect. The song that Mac Davis is singing on the radio came to mind. *"Oh Lord, it's hard to be when your perfect in every way."* Cute, but some think they are. The truth is none of us are perfect. Our imperfection is why Jesus came to sacrifice Himself, as only He is perfect.

Thelma is missing one teaching piece, and I missed teaching it to her. The Scripture says this about Jesus. **He made Him who knew no sin to be sin on our behalf, so that we might become the righteousness of God in Him.** (2 Corinthians 5:21). We are to walk and live the best we can in faith in God's Word. At the end of the race, we will receive His righteousness, as this is the only way we can enter into the Kingdom of God. Thelma needs to know that none of us are perfect, but some glorious day we will be.

As I rock back and forth, the wind whispers this question in my ear. What do I make of the "day that He hath made?" What have I learned from His creation? I find myself again, looking up to the stars, and the bright ones catch my attention, those one-upping boasters who grab their recognition reward. Then, the humbled, dimmer stars hold their place, shining their dimmer light in the darkness faded by the brighter stars. Living in their faith, they sure hope that some marvelous day, the Lord Himself will glorify them evermore. ***Blessed are the poor in spirit, for theirs is the kingdom of heaven.***" (Matthew 5:3)

<u>Snuffy Smith Sings a Hymn</u>

Come to Me, all who are weary and heavy-laden, and I will give you rest. (Matthew 11:28)

This past Friday was a busy day at Lively's Feed store. It is not to say that I don't work hard, but today, I had to work harder on Friday. That is okay as the day passes quickly, which Fridays tend to do, but Friday last was even quicker. I suppose the business resulted from the colder weather blowing down from the mountain pass into the valley of the Greenbrier here in the Almost Heaven. Tom is preparing for the coming winter months and bought some extra hay last week, which is already gone. The farm folks with livestock to feed came and bought all that we had. I spent most of the day carrying hay from the store loft to the pickup trucks in the parking lot.

On Saturday, I could not escape the saved chores that the little woman had to gather up for me to complete. So I spent most of my Saturday mending the fence around the garden and then a little hoeing around the Pea Meteors. Then, we went to the woodpile to chop wood for the iron stove and the fireplace. Shortly after, I found myself sitting in the old rocker and went into the living room to lie on the floor. I may have over-exercised the small of my back with the ax.

Sunday is always good and starts with a brisk walk to the Church on the Knoll. It was an amazing service that we had there with our Church family under the leadership of Brother Simms. Brother Simms gave his usual insightful message from God's Word but suffered difficulties towards the end of the service. Right after the offering, the door of the Church opened, and in came Barney Smith, who everyone calls Snuffy Smith after the funnies in the Ballengee Record.

I hadn't seen Snuffy in a while, or should I better say that I hadn't spoken to him. The last time we spoke was when Amos and I stopped to give him aid when he had a flat tire at Pence Springs. We ended up driving Snuffy home as he had a few too many Falstaffs.

I have known Snuffy since High School; he was an okay chum back then. He and two other friends and I would take up a collection during the week, and on the weekend, one of them would go to Caleb Hodges and get a quart of his homemade shine. On Friday nights, we all would go to the War Memorial Park, sip Shine, and listen to Hank Williams songs played by the older boys. They called themselves the "Trotters of Twilight." Sometimes, they would break into some Flatt and Scruggs, which was good, but I liked Hank, as he was the bluest of the blue. Once, my older brother got to go and see Hank and the Drifting Cowboys.

One evening, I came home from a shining night and was met by my father. It was a quick trip to the woodshed, and the willow branch raised some serious welts on my backside. I slept on my stomach that night, only to be woken up at 5 in the morning. Dad said we had hay to bail and to get up. I rolled over to sit up, but my backside couldn't take it, so I stood up, and my head couldn't take that either. That was the last time I drank moonshine with the boys. They asked, but I refused, so I made new friends with whom I could hang out. I lost track of old Snuffy for some years until I saw him sleeping at the War Memorial one morning. I didn't at first know it was Snuffy, but when I got close, I knew it was him—my how he had changed over the years. My high school pal was in dirty, smelly clothes, and it looked like I had felt the last time I tasted the shine. Every town has one, and now I knew that Ballengee had one, too. A town drunk. All I could think was what a waste of a life Snuffy had become. Now and then, I see him from time to time, and I shamefully try to avoid contact. Snuffy was always a mess and always had his hand out.

We now have Snuffy Smith weaving into the Church on the Knoll and falling into the front pew beside Brother John. Brother Simms looked at Snuffy, and I suspect he felt that Snuffy was a lost, tormented soul. I was sure that was a proper perspective. Sitting behind me, Martha whispered to Flo that she thought Brother Simms should ask Snuffy to leave. Flo replied that some of the men should carry him out. I know Johnny Crawford and I would, but Brother Simms or John must decide first.

Every time Brother Simms started to speak, Snuffy would fall forward from his seat and say he wanted to sing. Brother John would pull Snuffy back upright and place his finger on his lips to signal Snuffy to be quiet. It went on several times, and then Brother Simms finally asked what song Snuffy wanted to sing. Snuffy slurred, "Jesus died for me." I had never heard of that hymn and wondered how Snuffy did. But Brother Simms had asked where Snuffy had listened to the song. "From Hank, Hank sings that song," Snuffy said.

Okay, Snuffy, you sing that for us, it is okay. Snuffy nearly fell out of the pew to reach the podium but stumbled up there. Reba Maxwell went to the piano, flipped a few pages, and began playing the music. Then I remembered that Hank wrote that song and sang it with the Drifting Cowboys. By now, Reba had played a bit; Snuffy hadn't sung a word, and we all held our silence, and Reba continued to play.

When Reba began to start over, Snuffy leaned on the podium and started to sing. I remembered the words as he sang them. *"When everything goes wrong, and it seems all hope is gone, I remember how my Savior died. He died there on the cross so this world would not be lost; Jesus died for me long ago.*" As Snuffy sang the first praise, he began to stand on his own, and by the last, he walked up and down the aisle singing to us individually. "*Jesus died for me long ago on a hillside far away. He was tortured and slain. God bless His Holy name. Jesus died for me long ago.*" When Snuffy finished, he sat down, bowed his head, and prayed.

Brother John moved over and sat next to Snuffy and prayed with him. Sister Mary brought over a handkerchief, and Snuffy took it. Brother Simms gave a benediction, and we all sang a final hymn. "Rock of Ages." We all then filed out of the Church as Brother Simms said thank you, Barney. I felt Brother Simms's way of welcoming Snuffy back to life was by calling him by his name.

I am now standing by the fireplace in my little cabin. I am twisting around, warming the coldness off my clothes and pausing to give heat to my aching back. As I slowly turn round and round, I smell the buttermilk biscuits baking on the iron stove. The snapping of the fried chicken basking in the oil. And mother Mary humming Thank You, Lord. Yes, it was an amazing service at the Church on the Knoll. I could not help but wonder how many of us proud souls didn't feel a conviction from the events of our service. Indeed, Martha and Flo did, maybe others, but none worse than me.

From high school until now, I have spent my energy avoiding being near Snuffy. All those years of stewing his brain with alcohol, living in hidden places, not one friend to lend a hand up, and not I who knew and should have offered him an offer of God's truth. How often we offer only condemnation, pitiful pity, a buck or two to keep him quiet in his pain. Should we not be the Samaritan and get down in the dirt with one and try to clean him up? Especially if we know them, know from where they have come, see where they are going, and have the key that might change their lives.

Hank Williams was an alcoholic himself and wrote the words to a song that helped set another alcoholic's life straight. *"When everything goes wrong, and it seems all hope is gone, I remember how my Savior died. He died there on the cross so this world would not be lost. Jesus died for me long ago."* Jesus went to the cross and died so Snuffy could be found and freed. I wouldn't even cross the street to give him that truth. Snuffy suffered until he had nowhere else to turn but to the Lord. I am humbled by the arrogance that kept me from sharing that truth.

The Loyalty of Hank

Today has been another small but significant day here in the Almost Heaven of Ballengee. It's been a fine Sunday, and after our worship service, the wife and kids made their trip back to the Cabin in the Meadow. I decided to remain here and went down to sit along the bank of the Greenbrier River to muse over the weekend and events. I enjoy sitting by the river, as its rhythm suits the flow of my pondering. There is a certain peace in the rush of the water gliding over the rocks, creating a wave of miniature bubbling foam racing to the shore. As I look into the stillness of the water along the bank, I see the minnow society in the peace of the pools they live in. The smaller world has all the bounty to support their lives beneath the cool mountain breeze. I am surprised to look across the far shore and see a raccoon washing a fair-sized catfish for his dinner. The swoosh of an unnamed bird falling to grab an unguarded squirrel and carry him off to the lair of an unknown place. The view of the Greenbrier is a capsule of life: life being lived, life being used, and life in its fullness. It is as if it was meant to be lived to ever regenerate to the next page of the history before us.

I can't help but spend my Sunday afternoon sorting through the events of Saturday just past: the adventure, the drama, and the reasoning. The question must be resolved, as all under the sun has a purpose. God sits upon His throne, directing all the happenings of His creation, fulfilling His purpose according to His will. The question for me has never been if God's will be done, but am I living in it and His will? The day passed and left a question I did not understand as I lay to rest searching for the truth; I thought I had explored too much of the nooks and crannies of motion to find their reasoning. Sometimes, I become even more puzzled and exasperated as I search for the light to spark and reveal what is dark. If I have confused you, then you understand the place that I am in.

Saturday, Lacy Mc Beth, a small farm owner, needed to drive a few cattle to market down in Talcott. I've known Lacy since back then, and we have done some stuff together. He had a dream that I once had but soon discarded: to have a small farm. Lacy wanted a garden to support himself, a few hogs, and some cattle so he could have meat with his veggies. That and a few chickens and Lacy would be set for life. Lacy soon learned that he would have to do much better than that, as he would need some money to maintain and invest in his farm. There is also that problem like electricity and staples he'd have to buy. Lacy increased his herd and bought hay to feed them in the cold months when the grass didn't grow. As crowded as it was for him on his little patch of ground, it was working out.

As Lacy told this story to me last evening, the outcome was a surprise but understandable. Lacy has always been a calm person, or perhaps a steady person. For the most part, he is a soft-spoken man and was never one to get himself into any real trouble. The wildest thing I ever saw Lacy do was at his wedding to Mabelle Saunders. After the preacher had them say their "I dos" and Mabelle became Mabelle Mc Beth, all of us fellers lined up to kiss the bride. When Lacy's best man gave Mabelle a sloppy, wet kiss, Lacy round-housed him and knocked him out cold. When I woke up, I thought my jaw was broken, and I had a liquid diet for a week. My mom had to spend a part of her day liquefying my meals. As quite a man as Lacy was, I learned he had a firecracker of a temper, and I have always been careful not to light the fuse.

Now we are in August, and Lacy had three steers that he needed to get to market. The problem was that all the other cattlemen also had their steers to bring to the market. Lacy found himself with no help in driving his small herd. Lacy had a good dog named Hank. Hank was a pedigree mutt and was very smart and agile. When Lacy needed to round up his herd, Hank was the one who would do it. Lacy felt that Hank could handle driving the herd to Talcott just fine.

Lacy, Hank, and the three steers left on their adventure to Talcott early Saturday morning. Talcott was only a three-mile trip down the hard road, and all Hank had to do was keep the steers straight and off the hard road. Lacy would walk the lead and warn of any traffic that might come along. Lacy, Hank, and the herd made it to Talcott, okay, and he received the money for the steers. Lacy put his small fortune in his back pocket and went to the store to buy some needed things for the home. He came out of the store with two bags of sundry items and set them down on the porch. Lacy went over to the well, pulled his handkerchief out of his pocket, and washed his face with the well water. He gave Hank a drink and wrapped his handkerchief around his neck. He looked at Hank and said, let's go home.

Lacy took a few steps towards the road, and then Hank jumped in front of him and began to growl. Lacy told Hank to stop and let's get going. But Hank didn't stop and began barking along with his growling. Lacy began to argue with Hank, but he would not move or follow. It went on for a few minutes, but Lacy could not get Hank to cooperate or move out of his way. Finally, Lacy lost that firecracker temper and shot Hank with his pistol, and went home.

Once at home, Lacy began to think about how he had shot his dog and just left him there alone. Then he realized that he was alone too. Then he thought that maybe Hank might not be dead and should go back and see if he needed to be attended to. So Lacy headed back to the well at the Talcott Store. When he got to the well, Hank wasn't there. Nothing was to be seen but a pool of blood. Lacy found a blood trail and followed it back to the store. There, he found Hank lying on the ground dead. Lacy decided to take Hank home and give him a proper burial and picked him up. Underneath Hank, Lacy saw the money he had dropped when he pulled his handkerchief out of his pocket. It was a long and sad walk home for Lacy on Saturday evening.

It always amazes me how things do as they do. It is just a confirmation that God is active in His creation and is always teaching us of His creation. If people accept His teaching as the word and will of the one and only Almighty God, learn and live in faith in the lessons He is teaching, it will lead them to life. Rejection of His Word and twisting His truth by selfish rationalization is the path that leads to death. In the providence of God, Brother Simms was given the message today at the Church on the Knoll. Brother Simms spoke on a passage from the book of Ephesians. ***In Him also we have obtained an inheritance, having been predestined according to His purpose who works all things after the counsel of His will, to the end that we who were the*** first ***to hope in Christ would be to the praise of His glory.*** (Ephesians 1:10- 12) Our hope is found only in Jesus Christ, and the only way to survive this world and the next is through Jesus Christ.

Long ago, before sin was introduced into this world, we had the inheritance of God's Kingdom. Because of sin and because God loved humanity more than He hated sin, He sent His Son to pay the debt of sin, death. Humanity cannot accept God's offer of Salvation through the grace of God. Humanity is so shortsighted that they cannot have faith in the reality of the unseen. If humanity would place in their heart the eternal truths of God's Word and in faith live them until they are seen as reality, then their spiritual eyes would open, and they would see the inheritance that awaits them. But humanity is like my friend Lacy, who killed the one trying to lead him to his inheritance. The question of this day by the Greenbrier for each of us is whether we are still killing the one leading us to our inheritance.

Hank lost his life to secure the inheritance of his master. Jesus Christ gave His life to secure our inheritance. Jesus rose from the grave fully alive and ascended to the right hand of God to ensure that we may have eternal life to enjoy our inheritance. ***For this reason He is the mediator of a new covenant, so that, since a death has taken place for the redemption of the transgressions that were committed under the first covenant, those who have been called may receive the promise of the eternal inheritance.*** (Hebrews 9:15)

As I listen to the water flow over the rocks in the bed of the Greenbrier, the sound I hear is that of great power, power enough to fill the Gulf of Mexico and beyond. The Greenbrier is faithful and true, as faithful and true as Hank, who gave his life to save Lacy's inheritance. The Lord Jesus is faithful and true, and He gave His life so that we can have abundant life for you and me. If we do not follow Him and walk in His will for us, what kind of inheritance are we walking towards?

The Outlying Light

Sitting here on the porch of my little cabin in the meadow just up the path from Ballengee, I feel quiet in my thoughts. My conscience is as the evening of this coming night, and I think it is a solemn, sacred night. Today, I bid farewell to a friend I admired but never knew. His is a memory I have held close to my heart for over thirty years, filled with regretful neglect. I have always been amazed at how slowly Fridays pass, but the years fly like the wind.

So often, I console my flaws here, sitting in the old rocker on my porch. It is as the swaying back and forth addresses my mind as it passes from reason and emotion. It is not a religious or worshipful state that when my thoughts are cluttered, I look into the heavens to find the peace I need to discern. I have often been stunned that it is genuinely Almost Heaven here in Ballengee. As I look to the sky above, the numberless stars that shine down upon me are in the billions. The stars are not handicapped as in the city; their presence is unseen by the glare of the light. Only the brightest can be seen, and we miss the beauty of the dimmer stars.

Long ago, in a dimmer time that still holds the warmth of loving memory, I first met Brother Ricky Dee. As I have told you, Brother Ricky was the youth pastor of Grace Baptist Church here in Ballengee. It is a large Church and has a large youth group. Large Churches have more resources than small Churches like the Church on the Knoll. I went with Grace Baptist to the Billy Graham Crusade in Capitol City one summer thirty years ago. It was my first adventure from Ballengee, and it was just that, an adventure.

Brother Ricky led the group on the bus as we prayed and sang gospel songs together to pass the time on our eighty-mile journey to Capital City. Brother Ricky impressed me not only because I was a young, impressionable child but also because of his enthusiasm for the Lord. Unlike the scripted ministers I have met over the years, he sang with energy and prayed from his heart. My heart nearly jumped for joy during the invitational of the crusade; when I was afraid to go forward, I felt the hand of Brother Ricky Dee on my shoulder. I have always wondered how he knew, and I have always been thankful that he was bold and courageous enough to ask me to walk to Calvary with him.

Last week, Brother Ricky made that final walk up the aisle to meet his Lord and Savior. He was way too young to leave us, as he was only fifty-two years old. Today, Brother John asked if I wanted to go to his funeral. Typically, I would have told Brother John that I didn't care to go. I know that sounds cold-hearted to you, but I think funerals are not for the living. Funerals always make me feel guilty because I didn't take the time to tell the passing soul how much I loved them when they were amongst us. That day at the crusade was the only time in my life that I ever met Brother Ricky Dee. It is strange that our paths never met in a town of only 2800 hundred. It is no excuse that I never went to Grace Baptist and spoke to Brother Ricky after thirty-two years.

It does not mean that I am not aware of what goes on in the community, what is happening in the other four Churches in Ballengee, or the activities of the Youth Pastor at Grace Baptist. We always have an open line of gossip here in the community. Much of the reporting comes from my work at Tom Lively's feedstore. Of course, the Ballengee Record will print the facts about what we have already heard. Brother Ricky, over the years, has had a very fruitful ministry.

Brother Ricky was involved with Youth for Christ for a short time, but Grace Baptist could not support it. Not to be discouraged, Brother Ricky started a shadow program of Youth for Christ at the community center at the Lodge at the Bottoms. He had a program for the elementary, Junior High, and High School ages. Kids from all over the county came and were inspired to help the community of Ballengee and their needs. As the program grew, quest speakers, evangelists, and youth bands would attend the meetings. The High Schoolers formed a band, went around to other Churches and community centers, and performed gospel music. It did have a positive effect in Ballengee and elsewhere for the better. Idle hands get into mischief, but the youth group kept them busy. Brother Ricky called this youth program the Grace of Jesus. That is bold and courageous.

As the years continued to race along, Brother Ricky had an opportunity to purchase a campground on Zion Mountain overlooking Bluestone Lake. It was quite an undertaking, but by the grace of God, a way was provided to fund the purchase. Brother Ricky named the camp Grace Baptist Camp, and they ran a two-week program through the summer months. Youth from all over the state and neighboring states came to enjoy the activity. As with the smaller youth program, many speakers, evangelists, and youth bands participated. Evangelist Harvey Banks and his friend Preston Morgan spoke every Friday night, and many were revived and saved throughout the summer.

Brother John and I arrived at Grace Baptist early today. We stood outside, greeted the people we knew, and spoke only kind words towards Brother Ricky. In truth, I do not think any other words could be said of Brother Ricky. Brother John and I went in and took our place early, and it was a good thing as the Church was filled, and there was only standing room for the late arrivals. I was glad to see that the casket was closed. I never like open caskets as the viewing tarnishes the memory of an otherwise perfect picture placed in the heart.

The service was as much as I expected, with eulogies after eulogies. You learn a lot about a person at their funeral. I lived most of my life with my Father and Mother nearby. In my youth, I spent most of my days helping my mom with the farmhouse and helping my dad on the farm as I grew older. I lived not too far from them here in Ballengee over the years. But at their funerals, I learned things about them I never knew. I had a greater sense of pride for each after their funerals. Over these years, I had only heard of what Brother Ricky Dee was doing, but I never really knew his impact on so many lives. I know that for me, the tremendous impact was that he encouraged me to walk down and commit my life to Jesus. Oh, how great is that! Dr. Robert Williams gave the devotion that day, and the point he made from the life of Ricky Dee was fitting for his work in the gospel ministry. To sum it up, Ricky Dee was a gift to the Church, a gift to the community, and a gift to the many lives he impacted over the years. If the impact was as significant as the change he led me to, he is worthy of "Well done thy good and faithful servant."

Now, I am swaying between reason and emotion on the old rocker. I have come to some never-before realizations. The reason should be to control the emotions and not vice versa. I could be here with sadness, regret my emotions, and miss the peace of my reasoning. Here beneath the stars, set on their course by God Almighty, some bright and fixed with others dim and vague. Perhaps it is not the stars themselves but from where we view them.

In the city, there are fewer stars to be seen. They are lost in the clutter of artificial light, the glamor of this world. Just because we cannot see the stars does not mean they are not there. The stars at the Grace Camp are in the billions and all visible for the world to see. They are free of the glamor of life and free to reveal their truth. I have been told that some of the stars that we see are not there. They are so far away that when they flame out, it still takes years for their light to travel here. That is interesting to me and its relationship to us and the life we live.

When I ponder the friend I have never known beyond a memory, Brother Ricky Dee, I realize the truth that Dr. Robert Williams made about Ricky Dee. Brother Ricky Dee lived his life as a star from God, a good thing given to many lonely youths searching for a light in the glamor of this world. Ricky Dee showed them where that light is. Over time, the youth will show other lonely youths where the light they search for is found in our Lord and Savior, Jesus Christ.

The light from Brother Ricky Dee may be seen for many years to come. Only in the end will we know how many people benefited from the light he shared. Yes, Brother Ricky Dee is a gift to us from a loving Heavenly Father. The light will be shared for many years even though he is now home.

Every good thing given and every perfect gift is from above, coming down from the Father of lights, with whom there is no variation or shifting shadow. (James1:17)

<u>Another Way</u>

Sparks shoot upward as missiles into the fireplace's chimney with each snap and crackle of the flames. The sound of this adds to the comfort of warmth that radiates across my chilled body, for it is a cold evening here on this Eve before Christmas in Ballengee. With only a slight ache in the knees from bending to form a resting perch, I enjoy the captivity of the fire. It powers the engine of my amazement. It has the same effect as gazing into a star-filled sky at night. The dancing flames of the fire enmesh the thoughts of one's process. It has always been a wonder to me, a fire capturing my attention and holding it until all thoughts from the prior season have been sorted to their proper page. I think finding these moments and allowing them to do their work is appropriate. So often, we allow life to go unorganized within and deny ourselves time just by ourselves. With the importance of the time we share with others, we should not refuse that same privilege for ourselves, the time we hold just for us and He who created us. I feel closest to Him when in the presence of the star-filled heavens and the warm glow of a crackling fire.

Amid the warm glow of the fire and within my heart, I relive the blessings of the day and prepare for the challenges of the morrow. The wife and tots have slipped into their slumber, shortening the time for Santa's gifts! I too, long waited for the magical moment by the Christmas Tree. Oh, the joy of shared blessings from the years past. Oh, the excitement of giving a portion to each. It is a materialistic moment that expresses our hearts' spiritual desire to express our love in providing a portion of our plunder and not accepting the gift as much as the love of the giver. A time-out is taken from our worldly obligation to pay attention to those we hold dearest. I also have that feeling of can't wait but have chosen to tough it out in the pleasant anticipation of the moment, here in the fire's temper. I am amazed that this radiant transfer of warming light began with just a match and has grown to such an abundance of flame.

I spent my day wandering the streets of Ballengee searching for those last-minute gifts, provisions for the coming feast, and that one particular thing I had reserved for myself. I am stubborn by my fickleness and was unable to find one particular gift. Moving along the crowded streets with the other procrastinators of this season, with bags of stocking stuffers and mint jelly, I enjoyed Lester and Fonda's Bottoms Gospel Choir. The visit of the Bottoms Gospel Choir was the main event of the town's activity for the past two weeks and, to some, a great annoyance but a great blessing to most of us. Though they did create a snarl in movement, we received a blessing from those who had afforded the time.

I would have to list Lester and his wife Fonda in the record as mighty, un-sung heroes of Ballengee and the surrounding community. They have been a part of us now for what seems always. Their story began in the not so long ago here in Ballengee.

Ballengee rests along the Greenbrier River banks and blossomed during the earlier days when the C&O Railroad laid its tracks through the area and built a maintenance facility. The railroad followed the river's course through the mountains, and its right of way widened at Ballengee to allow two tracks for the station and maintenance facility. Ballengee has, and to this day, been a farming community. The C&O created a short-lived boom in our community; perhaps the old money of those days still sustains us. The Greenbrier flows southwest and elbows at Ballengee into a more Southern course. The railroad cut its corner sharper than the river, leaving a patch of ground along the bank unsettled with the rest of the town. Sliced from the city by the rails, this area became known as the bottoms and remained undeveloped for a time. In the early 1940s, a large lodge was built at the pinnacle of the elbow. The Greenbrier Lodge became a leisure resort for those seeking peace from the pandemonium of larger cities. It caused some development in transportation and utilities along the bottoms, and the area flourished for a period of time. Late in the 1950s, the C&O closed its operations in Ballengee, and the location of the bottoms quickly died with it. The Greenbrier Lodge closed, and the bottoms were abandoned.

The charming summer cottages, long lawns of green grass, paved streets, small marinas, and the Greenbrier Lodge quickly became dilapidated. The summer cottages became run-down shanties and housed the elderly, the poor, and the helpless. The green lawns became patches of overgrown weeds, and the streets nothing more than a collection of potholes. The marinas rotted, collapsed into the river, and floated away into the abyss of the Mississippi. The Lodge began to sag beneath the burden of better days gone by. The bottoms began to breed discontent, and if there was a crime in Ballengee, the town constable knew the culprit could be found in the bottoms. This section of our community, once the crown of our glory, became an open wound, an embarrassment to us at our town's front door.

Eventually, Lester and Fonda Richardson bought the old Greenbrier Lodge. There was speculation that they would try to revive the Lodge and restore it to the days of its glory. They did make needed repairs but made no effort to improve upon it or use it as it had once been. We then felt them be eccentrics who needed a very large dwelling. Shortly after Lester and Fonda came to the bottoms, subtle changes began to occur that, at first, none noticed nor appreciated.

Lester gathered the elderly and sick of the bottoms and moved them into the lodge. He enlisted the unmotivated women who slumbered upon broken porches daily to care for the elderly and sick at the lodge. At the women's insistence, the men cleaned up the trash and debris around the bottoms. At first, they endeavored it as a burden to their slothfulness but soon realized the joy of caring for others and the satisfaction of being cared about. They found a purpose for their lives and began to improve upon their newfound purpose.

Lester went around the lumber yard and offered to haul away the shorts and salvages of wood that would usually be discarded. He went to the hardware stores and obtained unwanted paint, broken, un-sellable tools, and materials. Lester enlisted the men of the bottoms to repair or rebuild the shanties. To give them a fresh coat of paint and clean up the yards. Soon, the bottoms' whole appearance improved as folks became happier with the bottoms' cleaner appearance.

Lester went around to all the farms and convinced them he could provide a Farmer's Market at the bottoms and sell their produce for a portion in return. At first, only a few farmers would participate, but soon all joined in. Lester took the donated building materials, built a marketplace with booths, had the children of the bottoms operate the booths, and sold the farmer's produce. With their portion earned, he fed the folks at the lodge and those of the bottoms.

Lester invited the pastors of all the churches to visit with the bottom folks. Each responded and shared visitation duties to minister to the people of the bottoms. The largest church, Grace Baptist, also sent their choir director, the First Methodist sent their youth director, and Brother Simms of our Church on the Knoll holds a prayer service every Thursday. But it was Fonda herself, blessed with great musical ability and with the help of Grace Baptist and the three Maxwell Sisters, who formed the Bottoms Gospel Choir, which performs every Saturday evening at the lodge. Surprisingly, they pack the house.

As I sit at the fireplace, it is hard to distinguish between the greater warmth, the fire, or the folks at the bottoms and Lester and Fonda. So it was they, the Bottoms Gospel Choir, that I enjoyed immensely on this last crowded day in Ballengee before Christmas. Standing alone was one of those great blessings given to us now and then, but knowing the history, it becomes one of those miracles that some think never happens anymore.

For those who think one cannot make a difference, I say, Bah! As one man and his wife moved into our community with nothing more than a faith that all things are possible within God's Will, found that which was lost and discarded in the bottoms and changed it into a foundation for our community. Because of Lester's faith, determination, and refusal to leave a door closed and locked, those souls found along the bottoms who came into his presence now live another way.

The truth is what has been part of us for what seems always but again may have begun not so long ago. On another cold December day like this one, Jesus came into the world to seek the lost and discarded at the bottoms. A spark of Light was found through Him, and warmth has gone out into the world to fill the souls of men. Through Him, we have found our hope and received His peace.

By His lead, we have felt the joy of caring and the security of being cared for. Because of Jesus, life has become abundant by His purpose of living through us. It is that as we had chained ourselves to living in a passing world, now we have gone another way to living in an eternal world beyond this. I ask, as we celebrate His birth, God's gift, are we still mired in the trappings of this world? Are we content with that which has failed us and shall continue? There is hope, purpose, and the greatest love, as the Wise Men sought, and those of us who have embraced His presence have learned that we find it impossible not to depart to our eternal home another way.

Number Seventeen Maxwell

The snow fell throughout the day here in Ballengee. We usually dream of a white Christmas, and it appears that our dream will come true on this day. It snows here mostly just a dusting, but the flakes were thick and heavy. The flakes melted early on as soon as they hit the ground, but the snow began to stick as the day wore on. As the light of day faded into dusk, a beautiful blanket of snow covered the landscape. It was very peaceful in appearance, as if we had been cleansed of the past season, and now we're ready for the coming new season.

Christmas is a benchmark in measuring memory by which we gauge our life events, and it has always been one of my favorites. Yes, there are other moments of the year which hold this distinction. Birthdays, Thanksgiving, Easter, New Year's, and tax deadlines, but Christmas holds the most excitement. As a child, Christmas is unequaled by any other event throughout the year. Christmas is even more significant than the last school day before summer vacation. Oh, those seemingly sleepless nights of Christmas Eve that I laid awake with great anticipation. Then, deciding which was the greatest joy, the giving or the receiving, was hard. As I think back, I believe giving carries more lasting satisfaction in my memory.

The events surrounding Christmas are no less enjoyable. Going out caroling with the church group and seeing the look of joy come across the elderly faces of those who stood by the door and listened to our surely angelic voices. Checking the lights and trimming the Christmas tree with ornaments that became old friends, each with their own unique world as the years passed. Grandma always placed on her tree this ornament that Uncle Jack made himself and the star that Mother made in the early years out of tin foil, watercolors, and ceramics. The tree itself became a monument of our family history. How we labored to place each tinsel in the proper place and excitement when dad plugged in the lights, and they came on and filled the room, the house, filling our lives with the warmth of family love and the hope of peace and joy throughout the years to come. Christmas comes once a year, but each one adds to a lifetime of warmest moments shared with family, friends, and those of the world, each a new page read over again the next time Christmas arrives.

Christmas has come again to this little community of Ballengee. As the years have made their marks upon me, I see it not through the eyes of a child's anticipation but the eyes of a seasoned child's appreciation. I must say that I have been blessed with much to be joyful about. The meaning now of Christmas is far more profound than the joys of giving and receiving but more accepting the greatest gift ever received. As I look back on each page of Christmas past and take from each personal pleasure, I have come to understand the basis of tradition and its importance. I then want my children to have the exact wonderful times now and in their memories. How empty the future would be if we allowed our children's future to drift away from the root of the Christmas season. I remind myself each year that if it hasn't been the Christ we celebrate, what is it we are about this season? I have been blessed that Christ is always the reason in our family, but what of those without a clue? Yet I think they do and still harbor the curiosity for it, as the world has yet to escape the truth of Christmas.

This night, I gathered my sons and daughter, who are not such little ones anymore, and we went out to enjoy the season as we have over the years we've spent growing together. Walking down Maxwell Street and admiring the lights has become a tradition for us and many in Ballengee.

Maxwell Street is perhaps one of, if not the oldest street in Ballengee. Maxwell Street is not the longest of the streets here, having only seventeen homes, but it is in the exclusive part of town. The oldest families live there. All but one of the founders of Ballengee lived there. Today, most of our community leaders live or are from Maxwell Street. That being who they are, they found it a commitment to giving the fullest measure in keeping the tradition of each passing season. Christmas is certainly the greatest opportunity for all on Maxwell Street to show their ability to keep up with the season. It has become a marvelous sight to see as the residents of Maxwell Street attempt to equal and outdo themselves with the lights and Christmas decorations. So, most of us here in Ballengee make an annual trek to Maxwell Street to admire the results of their effort there.

We admire what we have seen there in the past and see what has been added for this Christmas season. It is an evolving process as new features are added to the individual displays each year. I have found myself wondering each year what more can be done and have been amazed that the creativity of Maxwell Street has seemingly no end. So it is something old and something new every Christmas season. It has become an event amongst Ballengee's masses as we, the town folks, stroll down Maxwell Street.

Though we are a very tight-knit town, and most folks know each other by name, I still hate seeing vendors setting up their stands on Maxwell Street. As we pass down, I hold my displeasure, as they are my friends from many years gone by. Perhaps the one I have known the longest of any, John Crawford has set up a stand filled with delights from his restaurant, the Kountry Kitchen. Betty Mae runs the local Tastee Freeze and has an Ice Cream stand. Imagine that my oldest boy would stop for an ice cream cone on a snowy evening. Lou's Five and Dime can purchase that last-minute gift on Maxwell Street. But it's not much annoyance, mostly just personal displeasure of mine, and more or less tolerated by the community and even participated by those who speak against it. But I do not allow this distraction to displace my attraction to the extraordinary glitter I have come to see.

We pass by each house each display, which now blend into each other. We are astonished by their individual and yet coordinated creation. I am amazed by this monument's uniqueness, creativity, and effort, as well as by its remaining and changing throughout my life here. As I walk, my children, somewhere in the future, will have the same thoughts as I do now. Yes, I say to myself that it is essential to have anchors in life such as this to bind our lives together throughout the generations.

I am particularly impressed by Judge Stone's display this year. He had taken a garden hose and lined it atop his house's gutters. He turned it on and allowed Ice sickles to form. He then placed small colored lights that blink behind the sickles, and the effect is incredible. Not to be outdone, John Thomas built a wooden frame in the shape of a Christmas tree and, with the same principle, made an Ice Christmas tree with lights embedded in the ice. The ice melted around the bulbs, placing them inside little cavities that reflected the colors magnificently. Each year, the residents of Maxwell Street never cease to create something they have never seen before.

Maxwell Street ends in a hook at the base of higher ground, Laurels Peak. Here stands the oldest known structure in the county. It is an exquisite Victorian home built in late 1750 by Landon Maxwell. He came here directly from England to establish his lordship in the New

World of the Americas. He and his assembly settled this part of the country, the far western frontier of the New World. At first, they battled and then befriended the Cherokee Indians. London's son Brent turned against his father and sided with the revolutionaries in the war for independence. He was banned from the estate, but he returned to claim the family leadership at his father's death because of the war's outcome. Brent's grandson Chester Maxwell rebelled against the Government of Virginia, and the Maxwell home became the headquarters for Union Gen. William Averell in securing the area from the Confederates. A few small battles were fought nearby, and he successfully forced the army of Confederate Gen. John Echols into Virginia. The most significant Civil War battle fought on West Virginia soil, Droop Mountain, was directed from the Maxwell home.

Today, the Maxwell home is a monument to this area's history. We don't call it the Maxwell home but that of the three sisters. They are the direct descendants of Landon Maxwell and the last of his family. The sisters, Reba, Rose, and Mary, never married and have lived their whole lives from birth in the upper bedrooms until today in the Maxwell home. When in town or out in the country, the Maxwell Sisters are treated like the royalty they've come from. Most of the land Ballengee once rested upon was their family's property, so we seemingly remain grateful. Number seventeen, Maxwell Street, is the last stop on our walk.

At number seventeen, the three sisters' home is perhaps the grandest of all the displays to be found here. If none other along the journey moved the soul of men, the exhibition at number seventeen shall. Here stands, as has in all the years of my memory, one illustration of the season. Not overcome in lights or ornaments but standing uniquely upon its own merit. A stall filled with a straw floor and nothing more than a manger with a child resting. In the corners of the stall, candles flickered in the crisp night air. Behind the manger stood the three sisters: Reba with an accordion, Rose with an acoustic mandolin, and Mary holding a caroling book. They played their instruments and sang carols to the newborn King. Their voices, reflecting the many years they had shared with us, lifted high into the heavens with honest, heartfelt praise. It was as if the angels had given them a voice on loan from God just for this season. As they sang O Holy Night, the earth stood still and bowed to the most extraordinary gift man has ever received. At the end of Maxwell Street, all who had traveled stopped and remained in awe of this glorious occurrence.

As the kids and I stood there with the masses in silence while the three sisters sang, I couldn't help but marvel at the moment's reality. I couldn't help but take the truth of the moment and this Christmas season. This moment, this day, this season, our lives here on earth are all enameled here at this connection on Maxwell Street. As we travel down the road of our lives, all the glitter man has added to this world shall distract and hold us only for a while. But as we reach the end, the truth in the manger shall capture our consideration and that which we must adjudicate toward our end. For we all shall make this journey, and we all shall reach this end. Let us hope, let us pray, that we lose not our purpose along the way as neither the wise men nor the Shepherds of the field, that we have come to worship the newborn King.

<u>One Gift</u>

Sitting on a rise of ground in a small valley hidden in the mountainous Summers County, amid the Dogwood's barren branches, stands a white, worn wooden building known as the Lost Home. Officially, it bears the name The Summers County Children's Orphanage. Being quite a mouthful for the local folk, it is called the Lost Home. Here, the abandoned, unwanted, unloved, or parentless youth are placed until they reach the age where they can care for themselves. Tucked away in the hills, the neglected, like the Lost Home itself, is out of the view of the more fortunate of society. As worn as the Lost Home may be and as forlorn as the children may appear, this is where their childhood memories are born, and their adulthood finds its foundation. The responsibility for this growth falls to the Lost Home's caretakers, Mr. and Mrs. James Ulear, better known to the children as Ma and Mr. Jim.

A blanket of snow had fallen throughout the day, giving all that could be seen a presence of purity as if Mother Nature had given her blessing upon the future event with the cleansing whiteness of the snow covering the land. With the peaceful contrast of black and white, the crispness of clarity between the two was, as Mr. Jim had remarked earlier, a picture-perfect postcard day. It is as it should have been, for this was the day before Christmas.

Christmas is a time of joyful bliss to fill the hearts and minds of children everywhere. It is a special day that lives long in the children's imagination, filling them with hope, love, and happiness. A day is given to the rewards of good behavior. That magical visit of Saint Nicholas serves the desires of hearts in want of a moment to live in the freedom of goodwill towards men. A day set aside from sorrows and worry in exchange for the blessing of giving and receiving, loving and forgiving, and the celebration of sharing.

Summers County, not one of the most affluent places, gives little more to one's needs. It is all they can muster for the folks who live there to care for their own, and few crumbs were passed to the Lost Home. Ma and Mr. Jim are a good-hearted couple filled with empathy and compassion for their twelve wards. They began early in the year to ensure this special day, Christmas, would be filled with joy.

Mr. Jim would go out through the county collecting discarded, old or broken toys, outgrown clothes, and this and that and the other. He expressed deep gratitude for whatever he could obtain and assured the giver that God would bless. As the keeper of the Lost Home, Mr. Jim is handy and makes various things, toys, and furniture, out of the wood he can find. To maintain the magic and surprise, he'd work late and store the gifts in the old milk barn behind the house.

Shortly before Christmas Eve would pass into Christmas morning, Mr. Jim was busy in the old milk barn. He made last-minute preparations before Old Saint Nick's visit. The wind had picked up and whipped down from the mountains to sing an eerie song as it passed through the branches of the Dogwood trees. Mr. Jim jumped when he heard a loud snap from outside. As he turned to look toward the sound's direction, a branch came crashing through the window, knocking over the coal oil lamp. A fire quickly spread as the oil spilled out of the lamp. Unable to put the fire out, Mr. Jim ran to the house to summon all the capable help. They all formed a line stretching from the well to the old milk barn with buckets, pitchers, and anything that would hold water. The wood was old and dry and was quickly consumed by the fire. Mr. Jim could see their attempt to put the fire out was futile. The fire raged on with a brilliant red glow beneath the midnight sky. The walls collapsed in a short time, and the barn was a large bonfire. As the fire burned down, the flames slowly disappeared, leaving billows of smoke where the old milk barn once housed the hopes and dreams of Ma and Mr. Jim's children. Ma and Mr. Jim filed the children back into the Lost Home. Being filled with the night's excitement, they were unknowingly aware that all of Santa's treats had drifted into the cold night air above the dying embers of the old milk barn.

As the heartbroken couple lay down to sleep, Ma and Mr. Jim heard a knocking on the front door to the Lost Home. Mr. Jim got up, put on his robe, and went to answer the door. On the stoop, an elderly fellow dressed in a long reddish-colored coat waited. Hidden in a bush of white whiskers and a wind-chapped face, the elderly fellow looked into Mr. Jim's weary eyes.

"Mighty cold night, he rasped. I saw a bright light in the sky from a way off. It made me think a warm place would be this way. A mighty cold night. Can I stay here?"

Mr. Jim motioned the old fellow in and explained the events of the evening. Mr. Jim then offered the old fellow the couch beside the Christmas Tree for him to sleep. The old fellow wrapped himself in a blanket with a hearty show of gratitude and fell asleep.

As the sun peaked out from behind the eastern mountains, long shadows began to grow across the snow tinted with the rising sun's red color. The tracks of many footprints were revealed around where the old milk barn once stood. A rooster somewhere inside the chicken coop crowed, alerting all of nature to the birth of a new day. Lazy wisps of smoke over the old milk barn rose into the air. The valley was filled with the smell of wood smoke, giving a feeling of warmth on this cold December morning. The squirrels began to dance amongst the Dogwood Tree branches, and the morning quickly woke to a brand new day.

Inside the Lost Home, children began to stir and come down the stairs to harvest Christmas treasures. Their commotion awakened Ma and Mr. Jim, who followed behind with uncertain hearts. The children began to gather around the Christmas Tree curiously. A little girl gleefully shouted, "It's Santa Clause! Santa Clause is sleeping on the couch!"

The old fellow quickly arose, embarrassed by being unaware of so many eyes looking at him.

"Santa Clause! What did you bring us? Where are our gifts?" An anxious boy asked.

Mr. Jim stepped forward to rescue the old fellow but was halted when the old fellow raised his hand to command the attention of all in the room.

"I have your gift." The old fellow began. "I have a gift for each of you, my children. I have it here in my heart. Some gifts are for today. You have them, and tomorrow they are gone. Then some gifts are for tomorrow. When tomorrow comes, they are gone. But one gift is for life. It is life, and it will last forever. Some can only see today. They want only the gifts that today can bring. Their hope will soon fall victim to yesterday, and it is lost. Some gifts are promised for tomorrow, but tomorrow never comes, and their hope dies. Where are all the gifts I brought you last Christmas? Where will they be in the years to come? What if next Christmas never comes? What good is your hope for it? There is one gift that never fails. A gift never lost. It will always be yours. It is so great that you can give this gift away and still have it. All you have to do is take it. I have it for you now this Christmas, here for each of you."

As the old fellow reached inside his coat, all eyes excitedly brightened. He pulled a piece of paper inside his coat and laid it face down on the table.

"There it is, children, written on that piece of paper. When I leave, I want the youngest of you to the oldest to read it. If you want the greatest gift, the One Gift, then take it." The old fellow got up, bowed to Ma and Mr. Jim, and left.

I don't know what all the children did with what was written on the piece of paper. I know for a while; they thought Santa Claus had given it to them. Some, I am sure, felt disappointed and forgot about it. Others may have but, in later years, returned to it. For others, they placed it where the old fellow had kept it, in their hearts. As he said, it has been that other gifts have passed away, and tomorrow is always just beyond reach. No other gift they received has given them all they need, but His gift has. They gave it away to all who would take it and still have it, just as the old fellow promised. Yes, His gift was true, perhaps the only truth there will ever be. On that paper, it was written, For God so loved the world, that he gave his only begotten son, that whosoever believes in him should not perish, but have everlasting life.

There have been many Christmases since that day at the Lost Home. When I look at the universe's greatness and the tiny speck earth is, I feel the earth is like the Lost Home filled with unwanted, unloved, uncared-for, parentless people with no hope for their eternal lives. I believe God the Father looked down that first snowy Christmas morning and sent His son Jesus, who gave that One Gift, the gift of life, and all we have to do is take it.

The King's Stable

Through the universe, boundless as the imagination and bounded only by our vision. Traveling from the farthest expansion, an image, un-measured by time, which has no beginning and no end, crossed at the speed of thought, unfettered by natural law, stirring with the authority of the Creator; therefore, upon release, it existed. The image is fixed within the shelter of the un-violated womb of humanity, a virgin who would give birth to grace for humanity, a perfect lamb for our sacrifice, the Son Of God, the mirror image of man and his Creator.

In a faraway town, or just around the corner, or perhaps where you are now, stands a stable where man's beasts of burden are kept. The stable is not found at the center of town, where society plays the grandeur of its masquerade. At the perimeter, all pass at the beginning and end of their journey. The heart is a happening of many memories from ago, or was it just yesterday, or perhaps it goes on at this moment. The event happened without loud music or a great exclamation, but the truth is often kept in the mystery. So begins our story in a place without origin, a time without a point, yet it exists in the reader's reality of hearing and comprehending this tale.

Our tale unfolds in a town, the birthplace of a long-ago earthly King, during a busy time. An order had been issued for the people to gather and give an accounting of themselves. It was pressed upon them to return to their root and be recognized by the governor of their birthplace. They gathered and afforded themselves the festivities of reunion. They excused themselves from the worries of life and gave less for the concerns of the less fortunate. On the skirts of town, at the stable, it was not a time of gala activity but that of extra duty for Joel, the stable keeper.

Joel, a thirteen-year-old lad, was mature for his short years. He had a sense of his place and the significance of the events unfolding around him. He worked hard at his task in the stable in hopes of impressing the master and increasing his reward. Joel kept the stable stalls clean and ensured the animals were well-fed and groomed. Joel was busy, as there were many animals at this time, when his master Matthew called. Joel quickly ran out to answer the call and found Matthew bartering with a farmer for new hay to use as feed. Matthew instructed Joel to take the fresh hay into the stable when the deal was struck.

Joel carried the hay into the stable and stored it in the loft above the stalls. He had made room for the new hay by filling the mangers in each stall with old hay. Yet there was one stall and manger in the center left empty, with Joel's purpose, where he placed new hay.

Throughout the day, more animals arrived, and Joel put them in the stalls and soon began to double them, leaving the one with new hay empty. Matthew would see this and ask Joel why he left the one stall empty, and many a traveler would ask why their animals were not placed in the empty stall. To each, Joel would reply, "I am saving this stall for the King. When he comes, He shall be given our best." Matthew would reply that no King would come to this stable to harbor his animals, and travelers would reply no King would come to this town. Yet despite Matthew's impatience and the scorn of many travelers, Joel kept the center stall with new hay in the manger ready for the King's service.

When the day's activities ceased in the late evening, Joel checked each stall, comforting each animal passing the empty one. Joel then prepared his bed, offered his evening prayer, and rested. Shortly after, Matthew appeared at the door, calling for him. Joel quickly arose and answered the call of his master. Matthew entered the stable with a man and his wife, who was riding on a donkey.

"See to these people that they have a place to rest. They will require comfort here as there is no room in the inn. Give them a corner and their donkey feed." Matthew commanded.

As the woman dismounted the donkey, Joel saw she was ready to give birth. The man helped her down and led her to a corner of the stable. He unpacked a blanket and laid it down for her. Joel led the donkey to a stall and squeezed it with two others. Joel then fetched fresh water and took it over to the couple.

"What are your names?" Joel asked.

"I am called Joseph, and this is my wife, Mary. We have traveled here for the accounting. It has come at a bad time for us, as my wife is about to give birth. Our travel is slow, and we have come late. It is the only place for us to find rest. Why is it you have placed our donkey in a crowded stall?"

"I have been saving this stall for a King." Joel then looked over to Joseph's wife, Mary. She sat quietly in obvious discomfort upon the hard ground with only the cushion of a thin blanket. Joel felt a stir within his spirit and looked back towards Joseph. "Please take your wife, Mary, into the empty stall. It will be more private there, and the hay is new and clean and started to help them move their belongings.

With Joseph and Mary settled in the center stall, Joel returned to bed and soon fell asleep. Not long after, Joel was awakened by the sound of a crying child. He rose quickly to see if his help was required. Upon entering the stall, he saw the boy wrapped in cloth resting in the manger.

After a few chores Joseph commanded, Joel returned to his bed. Soon, a knock came upon the stable door. Joel again arose to answer the knock.

Joel opened the door, and before him stood three Kings dressed in the finest of clothes. The three asked to come in, which Joel permitted as he worried that he had given away the stall he had saved for them.

"Your majesties, I beg thee your forgiveness. I have given my best stall to a wandering couple. They have just given birth to a child. I could clear out another stall if you wish."

"That is not our request. Our quest aims to find this newborn child in the manger. We have traveled from afar in search of this child that we may bow down and worship him. He is the King you have saved the stall for, not us. We are not worthy even of His presence. It has been foretold to us that this child is the King of Kings. A King who has the power to save the world." The Three then entered the stall where the child lay in the manger.

Maybe now you say this story does have an origin, Bethlehem, and you may say this story has a specific time, the birth of Jesus. I would reply your correctness is not complete. You would then say, explain yourself, and so I shall.

It is a story of the heart. It is a timeless moment that began before the beginning and has yet to fill the age. In the Heart, at the center, is the place the King shall visit one day. He was there at the beginning and belongs there now, but He will surely visit there in the end. We don't know when the King shall call, nor do we know when He will abide. We do know He is the son of Love, and He is Love. We must always keep His place at the center of our hearts, prepared for Him. He may arrive with his legions in the sky, shaking the earth as all rightfully fall before him in fear. He may be the one who comes in a moment of need or who comes in need. It matters not. The question before you is this. Is the center of your heart, the rightful throne of Jesus, bought and paid for by His sacrifice, a fitful place for Him? The answer is where the story begins, and it is also where life begins and where life could end. Joel knew his place and the significance of his moment in time. Amid the pressures of the world around him, he kept a place prepared for the King. Joel kept his faith that the King would come and, in his heart, recognized His need and answered His call in the King's Stable.

"For today in the city of David there has been born for you a Savior, who is Christ the Lord" (Luke 2:11)

When The Angels Sing

As the song has been sung here in Ballengee, it is a wonderful time of the year. Amid the unusual foot of snow that had fallen this year, the streets are full of joyful souls popping in and out of stores, picking out unique gifts for those special ones in their lives. I was at Lou's Five & Dime earlier today, and the store was packed. Lou had gone all out this year, finding unique merchandise that folks could choose from to find that perfect gift. Lou looked happier than ever as she helped in the gift-wrap section, putting that perfect gift in a perfect package. It is essential as I always lose the argument with wrapping paper.

I also stopped at the Crawford Kountry Kitchen, and Johnny Crawford laid out his best holiday treats. I had only stopped to say Merry Christmas to Johnny but was captured by his Apple Walnut Cake. Macintosh apples and walnuts are baked in a dark brown cake spiced with cinnamon, nutmeg, and vanilla dash. The aroma filled a portion of the restaurant as I sat down to enjoy a piece larger than I should have, along with a cup of hot cocoa. Johnny and I had each spent the night before walking down Maxwell Street admiring the individual displays. So, while I overextended the welcome of my appetite, we commented upon each amazing exhibit that every home presented. Outside, we could hear the Bottoms Gospel Choir singing Christmas carols over at the World War Two memorial, bells ringing at the Grace Baptist Church, and the happy sounds of people as they moved past the restaurant. Johnny and I also discussed the evening's event, which we both were to be a part of.

From up on Eagles Perch, Nolan Richardson has a handsome sleigh that can seat eight. He has offered to let us use the sleigh this year to go Caroling, and this is the evening that the Crawford brothers, Johnny, Willie, and Bob, the Maxwell Sisters, Reba, Rose, and Mary, along with Lester and Fonda from the bottoms were to go. Everyone knows I have a monotone voice for singing, so I felt honored to be a part of this musical complement. This morning, I went up to Nolan Richardson's farm with two fine horses that Tommy Thompson loaned me, clip and clop, and brought the sleigh down to the feed store where I work. I spent most of the day polishing the old sleigh and grooming the horses to their best. It was all set then that we would enjoy a sleigh ride down Temple Street, stopping at every corner and Caroling to the neighborhood. Caroling was the first and maybe the beginning of another great Ballengee Christmas tradition.

As the evening drew near, the first to appear was light snow. I was delighted with this as I thought this would provide the proper romance for the whole affair. Willie came next with his banjo on his knee, along with Bob and his acoustic guitar. I felt a little music would help with my superior monotone. Homer Massy dropped the Maxwell sisters off, Reba with her accordion, Rose and her Mandolin, and Mary with several Carol books. Lester and Fonda came bringing some bells for the sleigh. That was a great touch; what would a sleigh ride be without the jingle bells? Then Johnny came, bringing each of us a slice of fruitcake to put us all in the season's spirit. We packed up and climbed into the sleigh, and I gave old Clip and Clop a smack with the reins, and off we jolted into the evening's adventure.

Thankfully, there was not much traffic out this snowy evening, and we could maneuver around quite well. We made our way to Temple Street and swung around to head up the slight incline. Along the way, Bob,

Willie, Reba, and Rose played their instruments, and of course, one of the songs they played was Jingle Bells. We gathered plenty of looks filled with marvel and admiration from the folks along the streets. It felt good to be doing something different that brought joy and happiness to our family here in Ballengee.

We approached the first corner, where we had planned to stop, and piled out to take our position on the corner. I started to tie the sleigh to a fire hydrant, but Johnny stopped me and said I should stay with the sleigh and tend to the horses. Somehow, I knew there would be a plan to prevent me from sharing my voice with the more talented company I was with. But no matter if I am a good sleigh master, I will be, and I stood ready to enjoy the first act of the evening's performance from the seven Ballengee Carolers. They started with a long musical intro to "Oh Little Town Of Bethlehem," I was amazed at how well an acoustic guitar, mandolin, and accordion could tolerate the company of a Banjo. But they blended extremely well and produced a uniquely beautiful sound that attracted a crowd quickly. As the folks on the street stopped to listen, others came out of their homes. Some stayed on the porches while others came out to join us on the corner. "Away in the Manger" was next, and folks began to sing along quietly. It was an extraordinary event to witness as the snow fell from the heavens; joyful spirits arose, carrying away the worries of this old world.

We finished with "Silent Night" and then loaded back into the sleigh to go to our next planned corner. As we began to leave, the folks around the corner started to sing "God Bless Ye Merry Gentleman," and Reba responded with her accordion. It was a moving sight as the crowd watched us as we moved on up Temple Street. It warmed my shivering bones as we trotted along with genuine satisfaction that we had done something to Bless His Children.

By the time we reached our third corner, people had already gathered and even had hot coffee waiting for us to drink. The snow was falling stronger now, yet they were there, not wanting to miss their turn. We sang, and they sang along with us, too. It was such a wonderful experience that I thought about what it would be like if every night could be like this. Perhaps it is in Heaven. When we finished, we wished everyone a blessed Christmas, and with illuminating faces of joy, they also wished us a blessed Christmas. The whole evening was as exciting and fulfilling as this, and when we reached the end of our journey up Temple Street, despite the chill in our bodies, we were sad that it was over.

I turned the sleigh around and began our journey back down Temple Street. The snow had stopped, and even clouds were starting to thin away, allowing the moon's light to glow through. Going down Temple Street required a different technique as, at times, the sleigh wanted to take the lead. I learned the braking on the rig and managed to keep the sleigh behind Clip and Clop, who would look back and snort at me occasionally. When we reached the street area that leveled out, we achieved a slow gate and a pleasant ride in the cool air of the evening. For instance, tonight, we had our first sleigh ride while Caroling. I was getting hungry and thought how nice it would have been to plan a stop for Christmas sugar cookies and hot cocoa. Soft cookies with brittle icing and little decorations like Grandma used to make. Oh, Grandma, she would spend all day over the stove making batches of Christmas cookies, and then we would take them to church and share them with friends. There was always too much for me, and I did my best to eat them all. Christmas is the resting place of many memories and the birth of many new ones.

Soon, we came across a dark home except for one light in the front room. It was Betty Mc Cormick's home, and I felt a sadness come over me. Betty had recently lost her partner of fifty-three years, and this was her first Christmas alone. I felt how awful it must be to spend this time of the year without the one who adorned you with all provision, shared every one of life's ups and downs, and warmed you on the coldest nights. I asked Rose, "Do you think we should stop and sing to Miss Betty?" We all agreed and pulled up in front of Miss Betty's house.

We gathered in front of Miss Betty's door, and Johnny knocked. The door opened, and Miss Betty stood there as a smile of joy exploded across her face. Near tears were in Miss Betty's eyes as she said to come in, please come in as I have been waiting for you all to come. Once inside, we stood around the fireplace and warmed the chill from our bones. Miss Betty came in with a tray with eight cups of hot cocoa and a pile of Christmas Cookies. The instruments started to play, and we sang 'Oh Holy Night", "What Child Is This," and "The First Noel." I couldn't hold myself back.

We stood there talking and laughing, and Miss Betty told of happy stories from Christmas's past. It was awe-inspiring to see this lady stand before us and share so much of the joy and happiness found in her memory. It was good for her that she had so much joy, and it was a blessing that she shared her joy with us. Now, the hour was late, and it was past time for some of us to rest at home. So we bid Miss Betty farewell and thanked her for her hospitality. As we walked out the door, she requested we sing one more carol, which we did, "Hark The Harold Angels Sing."

I find myself now sitting in a horseless sleigh at the feed store. The hour is very late, and I should be home tucked away. It has been the type of evening that I cannot, nor do I want to let go. Perhaps if I hold on just a bit longer before it all falls to memory, I can enjoy the reality just some more. I gaze into the night sky, lit with un-countless stars, and notice one that shines ever brighter. Could it be the star that leads me to an ancient newborn King? Or could it be a guide to a King who is yet to return for His own? And I wonder if the angels harold will come, as they did not so very long ago, as we have done in His honor this night. Christmas marks the day all hope relies upon and shows love has graced us both now and for those who answer for all time to come. Hark the Harold Angels sing, and Glory is the newborn King. If you truly want to bless the people, do so as the angels and announce the King, for He is coming.

A Day of Joyful Tears

It's early evening here in the Almost Heaven of Ballengee. I find myself sitting along the bank of the Greenbrier River just down the hill from the Church on the Knoll. It was Saturday, and it had been raining all day before the sun rose above the east mountain. I now believe the drops of rain are tears falling down the walls of Heaven, and early in the day, I felt they were tears of great sorrow. The Church family and I have been at the Church on the Knoll since after lunch. My family went home a few hours ago, and I remain at the river as the sound of the passing water over the rocks soothes my soul in this time of wonder.

Last Monday, Homer Massy called me and asked if I would take him to Capitol City in his antique Studebaker. I was at Lively's Feed Store and told Homer I would as soon as work was over. Homer said I need to go now, and I would be grateful if you could take me. I went and asked Tom, my boss, and without a thought, he said go. I then told Homer to come and get me when he was ready. I was surprised within five minutes, Homer was outside honking the horn of the old Studebaker. I hoped in, and off went to Capitol City.

It is an eighty-mile ride to Capitol City, and it usually takes an hour and a half or a little more to get there. Homer was quiet along the ride, making time pass slowly for me. Usually, Homer always finds something interesting to talk about, and we begin debating and end up in the far distance of our imaginations. Homer is my favorite person to converse with, as I always gain wisdom, learn, and enhance my perspective on various topics. Today, Homer said very little even though I tried to start something new, and Homer continued to look at the passing scenery.

We arrived in Capitol City, and Homer wanted to go to his doctor's office. When we arrived there, we got out and went into the waiting room. In a short time, the doctor came out of the room, and he and Homer went to a treatment room. Whenever I went to see a doctor, I thought the wait was at least half an hour. It may not be too bad, I thought. I sat there for about an hour reading magazines, which did not interest me. The doctor came out and introduced himself. He said Homer wanted me to go back home and come back when he called me. I was confused but told the doctor I would do as Homer wanted. Returning to Ballengee, I became worried and did not appreciate being left in the dark.

Tuesday was a catch-up day at the feed store, and when I got home, I was worn out. I spent a few minutes in the old rocker wondering about Homer but soon went to bed. I laid down and fell asleep quickly and was woken up just as quickly. The little woman let Brother John into the living room and came to get me. I went to the living room, and Bother John was sullenly sitting in my chair. I went over to the couch, sat down, and gave Brother John an almost nasty look. Brother John looked up at me and said, "Homer is home now." That is good. May I ask how Homer got home from Capitol City? Brother John said, "The Lord took him home." I was shocked, and tears were forming behind my lids. I Thanked Brother John, saying that I needed some time. Brother John rose and walked out the door. I hadn't realized how tired he was and felt sad for my counselor.

Today's service at the Church on the Knoll for Homer Massy was solemn and calm. It opened with several Hymns that we knew Homer would have loved. First, we sang "When the Roll is Called Up Yonder" and then "Beulah Land." I stayed steady until the last of Beulah Land when we sang, "Where my home shall be eternal, Beulah Land — Sweet Beulah Land." That should have been a lifting lyric, but still, it was more than my selfish self could bear.

Normally, Brother Simms would give the entire service, but today, Brother John gave the eulogy for Homer. Homer was born in Ballengee ninety-one years ago, and Brother John had known him for most of that time. They both showed up at the Church on the Knoll on the same Sunday and had been coming together ever since. I met Homer on James Street in Ballengee thirty years or so back. He purposefully asked me why I no longer went to the Church of the Knoll. I tried to make excuses, but Homer knew better and asked why. Homer was not a pushy person but persistent. He would keep going till the wall was too thick. He told me once when the wall got thick, he would defeat it with prayer. I never agreed to come back to the Church on the Knoll. I just did. Today, as I sit in the pew, I admit that the Lord always answers the prayers of Homer Massy.

Brother John gave the message from the Ecclesiastes, and I can't remember it even though it has only been a few hours. I was just too sad that I had lost my confidant in so many adventures over the past years. But I remember Brother John's closing thought with the following verses. The conclusion, when all has been heard, is: fear God and keep His commandments, because this applies to every person. For God will bring every act to judgment, everything which is hidden, whether it is good or evil. Brother John noted that Homer guarded every thought and deed that the Lord would approve him.

Sitting along the bank of the Greenbrier in the rain beneath the tears from Heaven being a despicable sorry me, I began to take stock of why I am so grieved. I have known Homer Massy for thirty years, and there are a few days we did not speak together. He would be at the cabin in the evening three or four times a week to chat over the days. Homer always sat with the family and me every Sunday during the service, and later that evening, he would come over to talk about it. My greatest instruction manual is the bible, but sometimes I think Homer wrote it.

I have spent hours here along the bank of the Greenbrier since the service today. I have treasured every memory I have shared with Homer and relived every memory Homer shared with me. I have felt a wealth of memories of the times we lived together. If I were to write a book, I could fill it with the time Homer and I traveled this world together. I should write it here along the bank of the Greenbrier, as it has always been poetry to me. Then it hit me: the last words Homer spoke to me when I took him to Capitol City. "Know this boy. When someone you love has left, you can be angry for the time you no longer have together, or you can be joyful for the time you had together."

"Precious in the sight of the LORD Is the death of His godly ones." (Psalm 116:15)

I want to express my gratitude to my Lord and Savior, Jesus Christ. His wisdom guided all my thoughts in this book. All Glory is His.